To See His Face

S. Michael Wilcox

Deseret Book

Salt Lake City, Utah

To my wife and children.
They showed me my father's pain and brought my redemption.

First printing March 1984

Contents

Preface

People have often asked as I related the experiences of my life, "Are they true? Can we trust your memory?" People who ask such questions do not understand life. Life is whole, inseparable and continuous like the flow of a river. Every event, from the greatest to the smallest, consists of three parts—the expectation, the enactment, and the remembrance. Of the three, which is the most true, the most real? However one answers the question, it is not the enactment—the event itself—that touches a life deeply. Only the remembrance can wed itself to the present and the future. Every act must turn within the memory to produce the wisdom and truth that become the expectation of new events and drive the life forward. In the memory the events can be lived again and again. The Lord can personify and expand them so that they never cease to teach, and thus we become our own living scriptures.

But what if the memory does not mirror the event? What memory ever does? We must ask again, "What is the truest picture?" If the enactment carries the truth, the memory carries the meaning and the power, for life has no depth until it is viewed through the lens of memory and given meaning.

I have tried to capture the depth and meaning of life and hence have written autobiographically, drawing on the experiences and truths I know best. I believe most fiction that aims at revealing truth and meaning will be autobiographical.

However, one assumes a danger when he writes autobiographically—the danger that readers will identify characters in a fictional novel with individuals in a real world. This book is fictional, and I have deliberately described no one within its pages, but have created the characters from the sum total of my life. In any given character a community of lives may be found.

I owe special appreciation and thanks to Ruth Cline and Skip Hamilton of the University of Colorado for hours of encouragement and critical analysis during the writing and editing of the manuscript. Thanks also to the publishing staff of Deseret Book.

PART 1

Search for a Foundation

Doubtless thou art our father,
Though Abraham be ignorant of us,
And Israel acknowledge us not:
Thou, O Lord, art our father.

—Isaiah 63:16

1

One-Strap,
Straw-Hat Annie

If you crawled behind the hedge underneath the principal's office and quickly climbed the fence during morning recess while the principal was in the teacher's lounge, you could duck into the alley leading to One-Strap Annie's without getting caught. The whole first grade was afraid of One-Strap, and I was no exception. Even the sixth graders avoided her. But every one of them had crept down the alley to the eight-foot wall surrounding her house. It had to be done only once in the six years of attendance at Jefferson Elementary School, but once was enough. It was everybody's initiation, and one I accepted as naturally as going to school. I had waited for my turn since Monday. Now it was Friday, and my heart was raising my temperature with its furious beating.

Nobody knew where One-Strap came from. She was as old as the earth her broken house sat on, which earth was older than any other in town. Standing on the dirt next to the wall could age you or turn your hair gray. A fourth grader had shown me behind his left ear the one white hair that he received by climbing the wall to look into One-Strap Annie's yard.

We didn't know what One-Strap looked like, but generations of boys had described her and named her. These descriptions were now recited with ritualistic reverence by the experienced boy with the one white hair. I listened and stared through the chain-link fence to the eight-foot stone wall.

"She wears bib overalls, but cuts one strap off, the one over the left shoulder; that's the shoulder they use."

"Who?"

"I don't know. It's always been 'they.'"

I received the information with renewed dread. "Is that why they call her One-Strap?"

"Maybe, but some think there's another reason." He didn't finish his explanation. We were hushed by the approaching footsteps of the principal. "Hug the building!"

I didn't breathe. The punishment for going down the alley to touch the wall was whispered about as much as the mysterious old lady.

"He's left the office again. We'll have to hurry." We scrambled down the side of the building and into the security of the alley.

"She never goes outside without wearing a straw hat," he whispered. "She weaves them herself. Her real name is One-Strap, Straw-Hat Annie, but it's bad luck to say her whole name."

I hardly dared say the shortened version. "I'll try to forget it."

"It won't work. She burns it into your brain once you've heard it."

"You're right. I can't forget it."

"This is as far as I go with you. Run as fast as you can, touch the wall as high off the ground as you can reach, and watch out for the cats."

"Cats?"

"Don't forget the cats. There's dozens of them. You can hear them fighting at night. When you're in junior high school you have to catch one on Halloween night."

"How do they do it?"

"Most don't. You have to go now. Recess is almost over, and we still need to sneak back."

"What if I get caught?"

"You won't if you run fast. She never goes outside the wall."

I leaped from behind the garbage can, looking back just enough to see a group of nervous first-grade boys trying to watch without attracting the yard monitor's attention. Their turn was to come next week. I turned my head to face the wall, now only five yards away. Before I reached it, the older boys caught me. Two of them had come down from the junior high to watch the first graders run.

"This your first trip to the wall, kid?"

I looked down the alley for help. My fourth-grade friend was already halfway over the school fence.

"Let me go!"

"You've got to touch the wall first."

I didn't want to touch it unless I could bounce off it on the return run. They pulled me the last few yards and pressed my hand against the stones. They were cold and wet.

"You want to see in her backyard?"

"No!" I could still feel the moisture on my hand.

"There's nothing back there except weeds and cats. Come on, let's lift him up."

"I already touched it. That's all you need to do in the first grade."

"We'll make you a hero, kid. Nobody in the first grade has ever looked over the wall."

I tried to run, but they pulled me back and lifted me to the top of the stones. I wondered how many hairs were turning white.

"What do you see?"

I searched every crevice of the backyard, expecting to see One-Strap behind every blade of grass. Weeds were everywhere, almost as high as the wall. I could see tiny cat trails crisscrossing the yard.

"I want down now! Please lift me off."

"Sure, as soon as we can, but right now we need to get back to school."

They were gone. I let my eyes race to the back door of the old house. The screen leaned against the wall, unused and covered with morning glory, the only spot of color in the whole yard. Then I saw her. She was coming around the side of the house, carrying a rusted rake and followed by a squabble of yellow cats. She had a wide-brimmed yellow straw hat

5

that half covered black stringy hair streaked with gray. One strap of her greasy, dirt-ground overalls was cinched over her right shoulder. The other hung limply, banging her thigh as she moved through the weeds. She was wider than she was tall, with arms twice the size of my legs.

I took this in during that frozen second when she rounded the corner and saw me hanging over the wall. Fear pinned me to the top like a beetle. Before I could turn around to jump off, she massed herself through the weeds like a boulder, scattering cats down the tiny paths as the dry weeds broke beneath her.

"Come down here, devil-boy!"

"I didn't mean to get on your wall! They threw me up!"

She hooked the rusted prongs of her rake into my belt and pulled me from the wall into the weeds. I knew as I hit the ground that every hair of my head was turning white.

"What were you doing on my wall?"

She pushed the rake at me, driving me against the wet stones. Cats gathered around her legs like a returning tide. One was missing an ear.

"I said, 'What were you doing on my wall?'"

Her voice was high, too high for the series of chins that climbed up her throat. My tongue filled my mouth; I kept my teeth locked together to keep it inside. I was looking for the leather strap I'd heard about—the one she used to whip little kids who were caught in her yard.

"Did you eat your tongue? Stand up and answer me."

I stood up, still hugging the wall.

"What's your name?" She stepped closer, and I smelled the onions on her breath and hands. A cat rubbed against my leg.

"Seth."

"Seth? What kind of a name is that?"

"It's from the Bible."

"What's your last name?"

"Michaels."

"What were you doing on my wall? I built it to keep you little kids out."

"I had to touch it. Everybody has to touch it in the first grade."

She looked past me to the wall. I knew she was staring through it to the schoolgrounds where the first graders were huddled. I could feel them scatter under her gaze. She looked back at me and drew her lips together.

"I'm going to tell your father, Seth Michaels. I'm going to tell him to whip you for climbing into my yard."

"I haven't got a father."

"Everyone has a father, and yours is going to whip you."

"He left when I was a baby. I don't even remember him."

"A devil-boy for sure. The kind of boy who troubles old ladies who want to be left alone. You throw things in my yard and kill my cats."

"No, I never have!"

"The devil's your father, Seth Michaels. You'll come to no good because you're the devil's boy. If I catch you on my wall again, I'll show you your father first-hand with the back of this rake. Now get over that wall!"

She picked me up with one hand and threw me scrambling to the top of the wall. I dropped into the alley, ran down its length, and climbed over the fence by the principal's office. The bell ending recess rang over my head, stinging my ears, but not as badly as the ringing of her words and the sting in my head. "The devil's your father, Seth Michaels. You'll come to no good because you're the devil's boy."

I often wondered if One-Strap Annie was right. I always seemed to be in trouble. Three days later I raced from the top of the jungle gym to the bars where three little girls were hanging upside down. I spanked each one squarely on the bottom with a ruler, then sped back to the jungle gym. My teacher caught me, and I had to stay in our room while the rest of the class went to the dairy to see the cows milked.

Mother had been upset with me that same morning when she finally found the abandoned crusts of ages of peanut butter sandwiches stuck to the bottom of the table. I had never liked the crusts and had discovered the bonding nature of peanut butter while in kindergarten. Maybe I *was* a devil's boy.

I lay on the mat in the empty first-grade room wondering what the dairy was like and thinking again about One-Strap Annie's angry accusation. I smiled, knowing I had lied to One-Strap. I told her I didn't remember my father, but that was a lie—yet, not a lie, more a secret, something I never shared with anybody, not even my mother.

It was the only memory I had of the first five years of my life. Everything else was blank, an empty night whose stars had blinked out one by one. If I didn't hang on to my one memory, relive it over and over, I was afraid it would fade like the others. It was my only link, my only beginning. Five years with one memory—the memory of my father and me.

I can see myself perched on his shoulders at an amusement park in Southern California. I see a blue sweater with a matching cap and a laughing face. I remember the rotating lights of the ferris wheel, and I am higher than anyone else in the park. I reach my hands down and place them on the cheeks of my father. He reaches up and rubs my hands with his own, then turns, and we walk off in the direction of the ferris wheel.

Only one thing is wrong with my memory: I cannot see my father's face.

Another memory came while I sat in the darkened room. I'm five, and we move into the house on Twenty-sixth Street, the one with the big red gate that looks like a horse. I jump from the porch to the gate and swing on it till it slams into place on the fence. I ride the gate for hours waiting for my mother to come home from school. My sisters usually watch me, but for some reason they aren't there. I puncture my foot on a sharp bolt protruding through the gate's bracing. Something tickles my heel, so I climb the porch to look—blood. Pain shoots through my leg.

"Mother! I'm hurt. I'm bleeding really bad!"

She's not home from school. My sisters aren't there. I can't put any weight on my foot.

"Please come home!"

I scatter blood along the kitchen floor trying to get to the bathroom. The blood won't stay in my hand. It's getting on the carpet. "I'm sorry I'm ruining the carpet, Mother."

I turn on the water in the bathtub and watch with rising fear the water turning pink and then red.

I can't swing on the gate anymore. Mother can't fix it as she did my foot, and Paul next door is too busy.

"Mother, if I had a dad, would he fix the gate so I could swing again?"

"Probably, son."

"Why don't we find a dad so he can fix the gate?"

"Do you want me to get married again just so you can swing, Seth?"

"No. That wouldn't be right. I'll wait for Paul."

Paul never fixed the bolt, so I never rode the gate again. For the first time I realized the emptiness my father had created in my life. I never thought of the first memory without the second.

So I turned to my mother. All the strength and security of my world came from her. She gave all without reservation, grateful to have someone to give to. I never questioned then—nor did I understand—the troubled look that often crossed her features. I never understood her pain nor the memories that came back in her sleep, the struggle for independence and self-confidence, the courtrooms of unconcerned lawyers, the embarrassed condolences of friends. I was young. I could forget—black out the memories. She needed to push them back, to overwhelm them with her love for us.

I did not know of the divorce while I was young, nor could I have understood it. She could not explain to a child what she was struggling to understand herself. I only understood that I could not swing on the gate again because I had no father to fix it.

I never wept over the memory of that choice she lived with for eighteen years until my father shared it with me. She never told me, yet she could understand him. She knew of his struggles, the war within his soul, and she could forgive—forgive him even as he closed the door and left her to a life alone, a rejection that mocked a temple covenant.

I walk the bridges of memory and see her trying to make a new beginning, and I want to remember, to share it with her. But I see only the empty night, the faded stars, and a little boy clinging to the cheeks of his father, watching the spinning lights of a ferris wheel. The answer, she would never—could never—tell me.

2

"When I Was a Child"

Sometime during my sixth year I began my search. I call it that now, though at the time I was not aware I was really looking for anything in particular. It began with my grandfather.

I met him for the first remembered time during a summer vacation to Utah. He lived in a house that he had built in Ogden. He was over six feet tall, straight as a pole, and talked with a Danish accent. In all my years I never knew him to wear anything other than a long-sleeved flannel shirt with the top button fastened tightly at his neck, even in the heat of summer. He had a closet full of beige pants all worn out at the knees and at least two sizes too big. He didn't own a belt, relying instead on the green- and red-striped suspenders that he was constantly adjusting to his shoulders and waist. He wore house slippers everywhere except church. His back porch was always lined with four or five pairs in order of their age. The oldest he wore in the garden, the newest in the house.

Grandpa's hair was whiter than anything else I can remember, and it blew in every direction with the slightest breeze. He combed it faithfully every morning with water that soon evaporated, leaving it to the mercy of the wind.

He had two loves—his garden and his books. "One for strength; one for thought." He spent most of his time lost in one or the other. Of the two, I think he liked his books the best. If he had been working in the garden, he would wash his hands with soap and scrape his fingernails white with his pocketknife before pulling a treasured volume from the shelves that dominated every room. Many of them were from Denmark. Each one bulged with tiny scraps of paper containing notes written with pencil in Danish, reflecting thoughts and questions he came across while reading.

If his love was books, mine was the garden. Each row was straight and ordered like the line of slippers on the back porch.

The first day I was there, he showed me the birds.

"Why are there so many of them, Grandpa?"

"Those are Mormon birds, Seth. They like to hold meetings." Over there is the Relief Society," he chuckled, "and that magpie is the bishop. See his suit and white shirt?"

I looked at the cluster of sparrows pecking at fallen apricots and then at the solitary magpie.

"Why are they the Relief Society?"

"Well, you watch them for a while, Seth, and you can tell. That magpie is wiser than a whole treeful of owls. He has to be to keep his eye on the sisters."

"Could I catch one?"

"Do you think you can?"

"If you showed me how."

He looked around the garden, then back to the sparrows. "Go pick a few raspberries, Seth."

I darted through the garden, then back to my grandfather with a fistful of raspberries.

"Rub your hands in the dirt to kill the smell. Now get on your stomach and crawl between the rows of beans over there by the apricot tree. I'll tell you when to stop. Don't rise up or you'll scare them. You just listen for my voice."

I crawled silently down the rows, wondering what my grandmother would say when she saw how dirty I was getting.

"Right there, Seth. Stop. Now very slowly slip your hand through the beans and open it."

Day-old cement couldn't have moved slower. I could hear the sparrows still quarreling.

"Hold still!"

Then the tickling came as the tiny beaks discovered the red richness in my hand. When the little scratches of miniature feet pricked my palm, I closed my fingers and felt the warmth of feathers and the furious beating of a tiny heart.

"I got one, Grandpa!"

I broke through the garden toward him, dislodging plants at every step, eager to show him the murmur of life in my hand.

"You didn't really catch one, did you?"

"You showed me how."

"But I didn't think it would—you really caught one?"

I showed him my fist.

"Don't squeeze her, Seth."

"But she'll get away. Can you build me a cage?"

"I'll hold her for you so you don't hurt her. You run and ask your grandmother for a shoe box."

I was back before he could move out of the garden. We sat under a tree together.

"Lift the lid."

I obeyed and watched Grandpa slip the bird inside. She bumped against the top and sides.

"I had a bird once, Seth. Kept him in a box just like this. A real pretty one, too. I was going to teach him to talk."

"Did you?"

"I couldn't."

"How come?"

"He died."

He looked down at me when he said it and rested his hand on the top of the box. The sparrow had stopped thumping.

"You know, Seth, it wasn't much of a bird, just a little brown nothing like this, but I felt bad. I felt bad because God knows when even a sparrow dies."

He drew in his breath and continued.

"I suppose even He felt bad. What do you think? Do you think He felt bad?"

I thought for a minute. "I wouldn't want God to feel bad, Grandpa. I wouldn't want Him to be mad at me."

He handed me the box, got up, and walked into the garage. I walked to the center of the garden, opened the lid, and watched the sparrow disappear over the fence.

Grandpa returned a few moments later with his knee pads.

"Did you let her go?"

"Yes."

"Did you feel God smile?"

"No. I felt sad."

"Why?"

"I wanted to keep the bird."

"But you did right, Seth."

"Then how come I still feel sad?"

"Sometimes doing the right thing makes us sad."

"Not always?"

"Just sometimes, and then you feel God smile."

He adjusted his knee pads and bent over the rows of carrots. He pulled a little carrot out of the ground and gave it to me.

"How about a carrot? I had to pull it to make room for the others, so you might as well eat it." He rubbed the dirt from it with his thumb, thumping it against his knee.

"How come you have to pull them when they're little?"

He took my hand and led me down the row of carrots. He moved the hose to water a new row, then squatted down by me and let the knee pads drop around his ankles. I could smell his aftershave.

"We pull the bad ones that aren't growing good so the strong ones can grow deeper and better. I won't thin this row, so you can see what happens."

I wasn't listening to him. I was still thinking about the bird.

"Grandpa? If you do wrong things, does it make you feel sad too?"

"Usually."

"Sometimes I do wrong things. I don't mean to, but I do them. I still wish I had the bird. Does that make me a devil's boy?"

"Heavens no, Seth. Where did you get that idea? You're God's boy, even when you do wrong things. He makes you feel sad when you do wrong things so you'll know you're His boy."

We thinned some more carrots without talking. He finally rose, patted my shoulder, and pushed through the lilac bushes that lined the garage, leaving me alone to stare down the parallel lines of carrots. I felt someone looking at me. I thought that Grandpa had returned, but then I heard him rummaging through his tools in the garage. I looked around the garden to see who was there. I was still alone. My grandfather's words came to me; then everything was still.

One night some time later, Mother came into our room and gathered my sisters and me together on the bed. "Your father called today from Salt Lake. He wants to see you and spend a day with you. I told him that would be fine. Tomorrow he'll drive up and take you to Lagoon."

Nobody said anything for a while, so I asked what Lagoon was.

"It's an amusement park with lots of rides. You'll like it."

"Will you come with us?"

"No, I'll stay here with your grandparents, but I want you to go and have fun."

My sister Jan didn't want to go. She didn't say so, but I watched her face. I could usually tell how I was supposed to feel about something I didn't understand by watching Jan's face. Mother talked us into it, though, and then put us to bed.

I lay in bed for a while wondering what my father looked like. I turned over and whispered to my sister.

"Jan?"

"What?"

"Do you remember what he looks like?"

"Like the pictures in the box at home."

"Can you remember him from when you were little or just the pictures?"

"I remember him."

"I can't remember his face. Everything else, just not his face."

"It's like the pictures, like you. You're going to look like him."

"How come I can't remember his face when I can remember the rest of him?"

"Seth, go to sleep. Tomorrow you'll see him."

She was annoyed, so I turned over and tried to go to sleep. The memory of the ferris wheel stole across my mind. I was happy I would finally have a face to put with it.

My father arrived early the next morning. He didn't come inside the house, and my grandparents stayed in the backyard while Mother met him at the door. I looked into his face. He didn't look like the man in the pictures. In the pictures you could see his teeth. Now when he smiled at me he kept his lips together.

"Seth, this is your father."

"Hi."

His hair was still dark. His eyes, which were wet as if they were about to spill over, were dark too.

"How old are you now, Seth?"

"Almost six."

His hands were clean, not soiled like Grandpa's, with a big blue ring on one finger. He wore a belt instead of suspenders.

"Looks as if you're growing pretty big. Do you help your mother?"

"Sometimes."

"What do you do?"

"Clear the table."

"Well, should we go? There're lots of rides."

I kept saying over and over in my mind, *This is my dad.*

We got into his car and pulled out of the driveway. I could smell his aftershave, but it was too strong and mingled with other smells. His shoes were newly polished. As he drove down the highway, he asked us questions about school, our friends, what we liked to eat, and a lot about Mother. Jan didn't answer any of them. While he drove, he tapped his ring on the steering wheel. I didn't look at him directly but watched his eyes in the mirror. They were still wet.

"Have you ever been to an amusement park, Seth?"

I remembered the ferris wheel, and the warmth came. I knew the man sitting next to me was the man in my memory, but the face wouldn't fit.

"Once," I finally answered.

"Where was it?"

"In California."

"Disneyland?"

"There was a ferris wheel."

"I don't think Disneyland has a ferris wheel. Do you like ferris wheels?"

"I've never ridden one."

"I thought you said there was a ferris wheel."

"I only saw it. It was night, but I was too little to ride."

"Oh, who took you?"

"A man."

"Your uncle?"

"No."

"A friend of your mother's?"

"No."

"Well, who then?"

It was my secret memory. I had never told anyone.

"I don't remember his face."

"And he didn't let you ride on the ferris wheel?"

"I rode on his shoulders. I held on to his cheeks."

Why didn't he remember? I looked at his face in the mirror. His eyes were still moist, and his lips were tight like wire.

"Did you want to ride the ferris wheel that night?"

"I don't remember."

"You don't remember who the man was?"

"No."

"Was he nice?"

"I don't remember."

"I'll let you ride on one at Lagoon." He looked over at me, then back to the road.

"And what about you girls? Do you like ferris wheels?"

Becky answered him, and then there was only the tapping of his ring.

"I'd like to buy you a present today. Is there something you'd like?"

"I like books," I answered.

"Do you get many presents?"

"At Christmas, if we're good. Elves in the light bulbs write down everything you do."

"Are there really elves in the light bulbs?"

I was amazed he didn't know. "Mother says there are."

He smiled just enough to see his teeth, then bit his lower lip and spoke a little softer. I could hardly hear him.

"Well, I expect you're good, aren't you?"

"Sometimes."

"Only sometimes?"

"Sometimes we sneak out of bed and peek through the furnace grill between the hall and the living room to watch mother watch TV."

He smiled again, only faintly this time. "Then what does your mother do?"

"We get spanked with the flyswatter. Mother says if we act like a pest we should be treated like one, but Jan hides the flyswatter."

"Does it work?"

Jan didn't say anything, so I answered. "When Mother finds it, she's not mad anymore."

"Is Christmas your favorite time of year?"

"I like Halloween, too. We build spook houses in the garage. How come you keep biting your lip?"

"Am I? Who do you take through your spook houses?"

"Only Mother and some friends."

"But Christmas is still the best?"

"Everything but the songs."

"Why not the songs?"

"I don't understand them."

"They're about Jesus and the shepherds."

"Not all of them."

"You understand the Santa Claus ones, don't you?"

"I'm not sure about Santa Claus."

"You're not that old."

"What?"

He didn't answer, just tapped his ring. "What songs don't you understand?"

"Why would Santa Claus kiss my mother under the mistletoe?"

"Where did you hear that?"

"It's in the song."

"Well, that's not—" But he didn't finish. He just tapped his ring and let his eyes spill over.

We arrived at Lagoon. He bought the tickets and watched as we rode the different rides. He never came with us, not even when we went inside the funhouse for an hour, but he was waiting for us on a bench by the exit door. When we were finished, he bought us each a book and drove us back to Ogden. Once again he waited on the front doorstep and talked to my mother.

I was holding the book about dinosaurs he had bought me when he noticed me staring at him. He bent over, brushed my forehead with his beard, and whispered to me.

"Now you be a good boy for your mommy. She needs you to be a good boy. Next year I'll take you to Lagoon again."

I went inside and waited for my mother, but she sat down on the step and talked. I tiptoed into the kitchen, climbed on the table, and watched them talking on the step. Grandma came into the room with a load from the garden. She saw me up on the table before I could scramble off.

"Greesabasa!"

It was a Danish word she scolded me with when I made a mess or did something wrong. I never knew what it meant. Her heavy frame shook at the shoulders when she said it, and the little stray strands of gray hair trembled above her eyes.

She moved to the kitchen window and stared out. When she saw my mother and father sitting together, she pulled away and faced me. She brushed the gray tails off her forehead, laid her hand on my head, and muttered, "He really believes he's done the best thing, but it's a strange way to love a child."

I looked up at her, but she was speaking to the window.

I was sitting in Grandpa's green chair reading my new book when my mother came in and pulled me over next to her on the couch. She had been talking to my grandmother.

"Are you glad your father came today, Seth?"

"Is he really my father?"

"Yes." She sighed. "Even though he doesn't live with us."

"He's different than the pictures."

"How different?"

"Sadder."

"Yes. Did you enjoy spending time with him?"

"It was fun at Lagoon, but he didn't ride with us."

"He wants you to enjoy spending time with him. He loves you very much. Do you love him, Seth?"

"Not like you or Grandpa."

I didn't know what she wanted me to say. A memory floated across my mind, the feel of his whiskered cheeks, but I still could not fill in the face.

"I like him, but Grandpa does things with me. He"—I couldn't call him Dad—"just sat and watched us."

She drew me a little closer. I wondered if Grandma had told her about me watching from the window.

"Seth, your father gave you more than a trip to Lagoon or a book. When you were little he would sit up with you while you cried. When your sister Becky was born, she cried all the time. Your father would sit by her crib with his hand through the slats and let her hold his finger. Sometimes he sat for hours when she was restless or sick."

I closed my eyes and pictured my father sitting with his finger in Becky's hand.

"Your father taught me, and in a way, you, about your Heavenly Father."

"Grandpa taught us about Heavenly Father and how He knows when sparrows die."

"I didn't listen to Grandpa when I was little. I did a lot of things I'm not very proud of when I was young. I hope you'll never ask me what."

"You never did anything wrong."

She stopped talking and looked down at the book in my lap. She reached over and took it into her own.

"I've tried to make up for the things I did, son, but I would still be doing them if your father hadn't changed me. I want to tell you that story so you will love your father even if he doesn't still live with us. We weren't sealed in the temple until just before you were born. Jan and Becky were born in San Francisco while your father was finishing medical school."

"I thought he was a teacher."

"He is now. When he finished school, we moved to Southern California. He became very active in the Church. Every Sunday he got up and went to his meetings while I stayed home. He even combed and fixed your sisters' hair so he could take them with him. I knew it hurt him not to have me with him at church, but I didn't believe in it.

"He started to read to me out of the Book of Mormon. I refused to do it on my own. I stared at the wall day after day, but he was patient. After a few months I looked forward to him coming home and reading to me, but I never told him. One day we argued about a passage. He told me God cared very much about all of His children. I laughed. 'If you're going to tell me things like that we might as well quit reading,' I said. There are a lot of sad things in the world, Seth, and I thought God had left us."

"Sad like he is?"

"Yes. He told me to go to another room and ask God if He cared. 'Nothing will happen,' I said. 'That's because you're too narrow-minded to try!' He made me so mad that I went into the bedroom and slammed the door."

She stopped talking so quickly that I looked up at her. She was looking out the window toward the garden. Then she began to cry. It was the first time I remember her crying. Then I looked out the window too because I felt a presence again, a homesickness that sat like a little fist in my heart. She started again, her voice distant and low.

"I knelt by my bed for the first time in years, and I asked God if He was real, if He cared."

She placed the book in my lap and gazed out the back window.

"Somehow I knew. I got off my knees and went back to your father. I told him, and we cried together. We went to the temple and were sealed before you were born. So you must love him, Seth. You must love your father."

I had to ask the question. I wanted to take it back when I saw her stiffen on the couch.

"Mother, what did he do? Why doesn't he live with us anymore?"

She was ready. She had decided years ago, even as she packed the borrowed suitcases to return to Utah and this house. Now the time was here. She placed her hand on my book and ran her fingers over the binding.

"I can't tell you, Seth. You must not ask me to tell you. I want you to know your father for the good he has done. We must remember only that."

I closed my eyes and saw my father and mother together on the couch reading the Book of Mormon. I kept it in my mind a long time. I put pictures on the walls and decided the color of the carpets and furniture. There were lamps on the tables, lots of lamps, and they were all turned on. I looked at my picture until I knew it wouldn't fade, until it had become a part of me.

We rose and went downstairs. Mother took me into the bedroom and put me to bed. I lay awake and stared at the dark place on the dresser where my new book was sitting. Grandmother's voice rose as I heard her talking with my mother. The softness of that afternoon was gone.

"What did you tell him?"

"What I decided when we were divorced."

"It won't be enough. He will want to know more. They will all want to know."

"I can't do that to him or to them. I know he still feels something."

"Someday someone will tell them. Then what will you do?"

"I have talked to everyone."

"They should know. You shouldn't protect him."

"Please, Mom. I'll never go through another marriage. He is the only father they will ever know."

Their voices became low as I finally went to sleep. I looked at my pictures again to make sure they had not faded, trying to keep the question away from them, but I knew it was still there. It would always be there.

Sunday, we all walked to the chapel. It was always hard to sit still during sacrament meeting. There was no air conditioning, and the building got hot; besides that, I had a hurt in my mouth that my tongue kept sneaking up on. I slipped from the bench to the floor where it was cooler and laid my cheek on the cold tile. We were sitting near the back, and from where I lay I could see through the jungle of swinging legs to the podium. I don't know where the idea came from, but I decided to make a dash on my hands and knees for the front of the chapel. I looked for a safe way through the legs so I wouldn't get kicked. Then I was off, crawling as fast as I could go, dodging the tangle of legs.

A ripple of confusion moved through the chapel as heads bent like falling dominoes. A few men made a grab for me, but I was too fast. I was safe when I reached the front rows. No one ever sat on them. I was so proud of myself for making it all the way to the front that I stood up, smiled, and waved at my mother, who was just discovering the reason for the congregation's confusion. She motioned for me to come back, which I did to the accompanying stares of three hundred people. When I reached my seat, Grandpa was bending over trying not to laugh. Mother was trying to look serious, but I could see the smile pushing her cheeks back. I knew I was out of trouble. Jan had taught me that if you could make grownups laugh when you were in trouble, everything would be all right.

Mother leaned over to my Grandfather. "It's a good thing it was here and not home. They would have been whispering for weeks."

I sidled up to her, but the meeting was still too long, and before it was over I fell asleep on her lap.

22

The next day I helped Grandpa stack firewood behind the garage. The sparrow Relief Society was still meeting in the apricot tree.

"It's homemaking meeting this morning. They're always quieter when there's work to be done," he told me.

I listened to him laughing softly and thought of Sunday.

"Grandpa, when people love you, do they laugh?"

"I guess they do. Loving and laughing seem to go nicely together, now that you mention it."

"What if somebody doesn't laugh?"

"Everybody laughs, Seth."

"My father doesn't."

He stopped stacking for a moment, turned and looked at me, then bent over the woodpile once again. Every log fit tightly against the others. Even the knots were carefully cut away.

"Do you think he loves us?"

"Why do you ask that, Seth?"

"Mother told me that he did, but he never laughed when we went on the rides."

"You don't always laugh when you love people."

"Just sometimes?"

"Just sometimes."

"He's not living with us anymore."

"No. He's not living with you anymore."

He placed a log on the pile, then removed it because it stuck out. He shifted a few logs and then tried again. This time it slipped into place. "But that doesn't mean he doesn't love you."

"But if he loved us he would want to be with us."

"Sometimes not being with people shows you love them too."

"It does?"

He wanted to explain it, but couldn't find the words to use.

"Maybe the best thing your father ever did to show you that he loved you was to let you live with just your mother. Sometimes it's best that way. People are happier."

"Is that why you and Grandma didn't talk to him when he came for us?"

"No. That's not why, Seth."

I waited for more, but he picked up a saw in silence. I watched him saw the end off a log so it fit perfectly. When he finished, he lowered the saw and studied the ground for a moment.

"Seth, you're asking big, grown-up questions, but you've still got a little-boy mind. When you get older, you'll understand what Grandpa is saying about your father."

I took his word for it and let the question settle into my mind. But as I grew older, I did not understand. I still had a little-boy mind.

3

Uncle Jens

Uncle Jens came later that same summer. There was some problem. Mother and Grandpa never discussed it openly, but it was always in their conversations. Something had happened during the War. When they talked about it, my grandfather got a stiff look to his face, his lips tightening as if trying to hold back some forbidden word. He wasn't my grandpa then. After their talks he worked in the garden, but he didn't take me. I watched him from the back window thinning carrots and moving his hoses. He talked to himself in Danish. Sometimes he sat for a long time and stared down the rows. I knew better than to bother him during those times. When he finished thinning, he would come back into the house, pull his Danish Bible from the drawer, and read. The stiffness would leave him, and I could talk to him again.

I never asked about Uncle Jens, but I planned to watch him and learn about the problem and why Grandpa wasn't Grandpa when he thought of him. If I figured it out, I could thin carrots again and be a part of Grandpa's world like before.

Uncle Jens came on a Sunday morning while I was at church. He became an obsession from the beginning. There was an empty space in me he moved into and made his own, and he pushed Grandpa out.

He was sitting on the couch in the living room looking at a magazine. His eyes flew over the pages as if he were looking at a picture book. My mother had told me that he was very smart, something about a valedictorian. I didn't know what it meant except that it made Grandpa proud.

He stood up when we entered the room and greeted my mother. She kissed him on the cheek and told him he had lost more weight since the last time she saw him. I was afraid of him because of Grandpa's stiffness and because he was taller than Grandpa.

He stepped over to us slowly and deliberately with a heaviness that made me think he had weights on his legs. They seemed to swim in his trousers and pull his body reluctantly after them. He had black hair that he pulled straight back over his head. It was cut short and always had a wet look about it, as though he had just stepped from the shower. It wasn't a clean look, just a wet one. His eyes were as dark as his hair and lay deep in his sockets; they didn't seem to move. When he looked, he moved his head. His face was longer than normal, and his cheeks seemed to go on forever before they ended abruptly at his chin. They made little hollows on his face. I thought he had something in his throat that pulled at them with invisible strings. His face looked unshaven, even in the morning. He was the first person I could remember down to the last detail.

He spoke to my sisters first, then reached out to ruffle my hair. It was then I noticed the smell. It wasn't an unpleasant odor, just different. It made me think of old buildings and cellars. I had smelled it before, but I didn't know where. It seemed to come from all over him. It came from his hand as he reached out to touch me and from his clothes as I followed him into the kitchen for dinner.

He had long, thin fingers that moved almost mechanically, and he wore a ring on one of them. I watched it dip and rise as he picked through his dinner. After dinner he stretched his hands behind his neck and interlaced his fingers. Halfway through dinner I noticed my grandfather watching me.

I didn't talk to Uncle Jens much that first day, and Jan and Becky didn't like to be around him. I learned he had been a bombardier during the war and had flown missions over Germany. He had been awarded some kind of medal. In Grandpa's desk was an old photograph of him with his uniform on. I didn't know where he lived or how long he was going to stay. Mother talked to him more than Grandpa, who spent most of his time in the garden moving hoses and thinning.

On the third day of his visit my grandmother called my mother away, leaving me alone in the room with him. He was standing by the green rocking chair. I became aware of his eyes on me. I could see his hands moving, working a coaster picked up from the coffee table.

"It looks like your grandfather has been talking to you. You've been reading for over an hour. Is it interesting?"

I turned and looked up at him. He was smiling. "Yes, Uncle Jens. I like to read."

His fingers spun the coaster. "Your grandpa did the same thing to me. I read all the books in the house before I was sixteen."

He motioned to the many bookcases, then sat down next to me and picked up my book. The odor came back again, and I tried to place it, but couldn't. I loosened up more and more and asked him questions about flying airplanes. We talked for half an hour, reliving his bombing missions over Germany, his decorations, and the end of the war. I found myself liking him, forgetting the smell and the sight of my grandfather stooped over in the garden moving up and down the carrot patches.

Suddenly he got up. "I need to go now, Seth."

He did that often, leaving in the middle of a conversation or a television program. He went outside, down the sidewalk, and around the corner out of sight. He was gone for an hour.

Grandpa moved the hoses, and I sat on the kitchen chair waiting for him to come back.

"I'll make you an airplane," he said one day.

He stretched his long arm toward the writing table and pulled out a pad of typing paper. "I flew in a lot of different airplanes during the war. I'll show you what they looked like."

He curled his fingers around the paper and began to fold it. I watched in fascination as he worked the paper into different positions, folding it one way, then making little cuts with his pocketknife. He tore off a few pieces, and an airplane took shape. It took him ten minutes to make an airplane and hand it to me.

"Here. What do you think of that?"

"It looks like a model I saw in the store!"

"Here's where the gunner sat. He could rotate himself to any position to fire at the enemy. Once we were hit with enemy fire about here."

I watched his cheeks sink deeper into his mouth.

"The bombs were stored in here. When I pulled a little knob on the inside of the plane, these doors opened and the bombs dropped."

He folded a miniature bomb, placed it inside the airplane, and opened the doors to show me how it worked.

"Here, I'll make you another one." He took another piece of paper and began to fold and cut again.

"This is a fighter plane, Seth. These are the flaps, and this is the cockpit. Use the coffee table as a runway."

I took off and landed, maneuvering the paper airplanes according to his directions.

"I need to go now, Seth."

"Can I go with you?"

"No, but you can keep the airplanes. I'll be back, and we'll make some more."

After that I didn't mind the smell or his frequent walks around the corner. In the days that followed he made me many airplanes. I had so many I didn't know where to keep them and was afraid my grandmother would throw them away. She thought they were senseless and mumbled in Danish when she saw Uncle Jens making them for me.

"As soon as I finish this transport plane," he whispered, "we'll make some hangars so your grandma won't throw them away."

We went out to the garage. Grandpa was sorting through the tiny drawers he had made, looking for bolts and washers. He stopped when he saw us and watched as we picked up two cardboard boxes. We returned to the house, and Uncle Jens made the exact cuts for the door and windows. He attached some shoe boxes for the smaller planes and made a landing pad for a helicopter he was going to make for me. We placed the planes in the hangars and moved them to the basement.

He left that night while I was asleep. He never told me he was going. No one explained it to me, even when I asked, but everyone seemed happier when he was gone. I wandered out into the garden for the first time in days and watched my grandfather work down the rows with the knee pads looped around his legs. He looked up and saw me standing by the woodpile.

"I haven't seen you in the garden for quite a while, Seth. The sisters over there have missed you." He chuckled as he said it. It seemed like a new sound. "Where have you been keeping yourself?"

It was hard for me to tell him I had been with Uncle Jens. "I've been playing in the house, mostly."

He turned and focused his attention on the garden once again. "Have you been reading in the house, Seth?"

I stepped through the rows to where he was working and squatted down beside him. "I've been making planes with Uncle Jens."

"Ah."

"He left this morning before I woke up."

"Yes, I know. Do you miss him?"

"No, Grandpa. I don't miss him." I wasn't sure. I felt that's what he wanted to hear.

He stopped thinning carrots, adjusted the shoulder straps of his suspenders, and stood up. "You're going home in a few days, so maybe we should dig up your section of carrots."

He got the fork from the garage. I knelt on the ground next to the row. He lifted the fork and spilled the carrots in a heap in front of me, then stooped next to me and cleared away the dirt. The carrots were all stunted dwarfs, twisted around each other into strange corkscrews. I looked in amazement into my grandfather's face and saw him smile.

"They grow deeper and straighter when they have room to grow, but they can't do that when they're too close together. That's why we thin them."

Uncle Jens was often in my thoughts, but I saw him only one more time, two summers later just before he died. I almost missed him the year he died because Mother wanted me to spend the summer at my Uncle Morgan's ranch in Nevada. I had been there only a week when I heard that Uncle Jens was sick. Aunt Pearl, his sister, was going to drive to Ogden to see him. I felt uncomfortable all alone at the ranch and asked if I could go with her and see Grandpa.

On the way I talked to my aunt about Uncle Jens. She explained to me that I probably wouldn't be able to see him. "He's very sick, Seth." She couldn't explain what it was he had, just that he wouldn't live very long.

When we arrived in Ogden I asked Grandpa if I could see Uncle Jens.

"He's resting in bed now, Seth, and won't be up for a few hours. Would you like to come with me to the garden?"

"I'll wait here until he wakes up."

Everyone went outside. I sat on the couch we used to talk and play on and watched the hallway leading to his room. I sat and waited, fearing that this would be the last meeting. The empty space inside me seemed to swell and fill the house.

Nobody knew I talked to him. They were still outside when the door finally opened.

When I saw him I wanted to run, run to the garden and my grandfather. But my eyes refused to shut out the sight of the hollow specter that moved from the bedroom and labored down the hallway. He rested at the corner of the hall, braced himself against the wall, then dragged himself the last few feet into the light of the living room.

"Uncle Jens?"

His cheeks were drawn deeper into his face.

"Do you need some help?"

The sound seemed to take minutes to reach him. I was afraid he would fall to the floor and I would have to run past him to get help.

"Grandpa, Uncle Jens needs help!"

Nobody answered. The smell was so strong I could feel it coming from him toward me like a vapor. He turned his head in my direction, and his puzzled expression held me to my seat, demanding that I write the memory.

"It's Seth, Uncle Jens."

His head moved across the span of the couch, searching for the voice. I looked far back into his forehead to find his eyes, no longer black, but a pale, colorless gray like his face and his hands, which hung listlessly at his sides.

He moved into the room and sat in Grandpa's rocking chair. I was a few feet away from him.

"Uncle Jens? Do you want me to get someone?"

He took a long time to answer, finally drawing the words from deep in his chest and forcing them through the drawn lips.

"No, I don't want anything."

He began to cough. He opened his eyes wide and stared at me, going over every inch of my face, trying to order it in his confusion.

"It's Seth."

"Seth?"

"You used to make airplanes for me."

"I flew a lot of airplanes."

"You made them for me."

"I flew airplanes."

"Please remember. You made hangars for me. We cut doors in them for the airplanes. The coffee table was the runway."

His lips loosened up long enough to allow the hint of a smile to escape. He was remembering.

"Seth. Do you still read like you used to?"

"Yes, Uncle Jens."

"That's good. You should always read. You should be like your Grandpa."

I could feel the question forming within me. Something pushed it out and hung it there in the air between us.

"What's the matter with you, Uncle Jens?"

"Still asking questions, Seth? You were always asking questions. Sometimes they get you in trouble."

He looked at his hands lying in his lap. "I'll tell you Seth. I'm—"

He couldn't finish. He looked up from his lap into my face, then let his head sag onto his chest. I was silent.

"You don't want to be like me, Seth." His voice changed. "I'm a drunk, not a war hero, just a drunk who's going to die."

His voice echoed in my ears.

"I need to leave, Uncle Jens!"

He was lost again in his own world. His eyes narrowed as he wrestled the thoughts into words. "Did I ever make you that helicopter, Seth?"

I couldn't say anything. My lips were as tight as his.

"Bring me a piece of paper from the desk. I'll make you that helicopter."

Unseen hands helped me up and led me to the desk. I opened the drawer and saw the pad of typing paper my grandmother always kept for letters. I handed him the paper and watched as his hands tried to close around it, those hands I never wanted to forget.

I didn't look at his face again, just his hands desperately trying to fold a piece of paper in half. Hands that once had never stopped moving, never rested, now trembled in frustration. They wrinkled and tore the paper, refusing to admit a reality that an eight-year-old boy could see and now understand. I stood at his side and watched his shaking fingers and cried and let the tears fall on the green arm of my grandfather's rocking chair.

"Don't cry, Seth."

I reached out and touched him. For the first time in my life I touched him and felt the cold, hairless skin of his arm. I touched his hand and pulled the paper from his tortured fingers and watched them fall into the hollow that was his lap and lie still.

I looked at the torn remains of the paper and thought of a box lying deep in a closet downstairs and knew I would never look in it again. I dropped the paper and looked one last time at those hands I had learned to love and saw the tears fall on them. They were his tears now, shed too late. I left him in the chair and found my grandfather. Without asking a question, he showed me how to move the hoses. We moved them together until the garden was flooded. When Uncle Jens died shortly thereafter, we were still moving hoses.

4

Like Aspens in the Wind

Many others after Uncle Jens dotted my childhood. I sought them out and demanded more of them than they could give, more than anyone could give. I made each of them my potential father. So many teachers talked about families in the eternities.

"Who will my father be when I die?"

"You'll live with God."

"And be sealed to Him like others in the temple?"

"Not like that."

"Then who?"

I never got an answer, only a hint of a source that could fill the hunger. I had felt a presence before, the smile of God, as Grandpa explained.

"Grandpa, I feel strange sometimes when I'm in the garden, like somebody's watching me."

"Remember the story of Samuel, Seth?"

"He was a prophet."

"He was a little boy, too. Think of the sparrow when you feel that way again and listen inside you."

I wanted more.

"I've never heard anything, Grandpa."

"Soon you will hear its whisper."

Before my eighth birthday we began talking about baptism in Primary. I was anxious about my baptism because I hadn't been the best boy in church. There had been some truth in One-Strap Annie's accusations, and every time I got in trouble I remembered. During Sunday School I spent my time shooting rubber bands over the heads of the other class members. I got caught one day.

"Sister Michaels, Seth doesn't seem able to control himself in his Sunday School class." It was the first counselor in the bishopric. "We think he should sit in your class for a while."

Mother taught the Parent and Child Relations class. I sat in there for three weeks before they let me back into my own. That's when the whispering started, and my dim future was predicted by concerned ward members.

"He needs a father," I heard a ward member say to her. "You should remarry."

"You don't know my son, Sister Williams."

"And the bottles? You need to be careful with him."

I had stolen pop bottles from all the neighbors in my greed for enough money to buy baseball cards. Sister Williams lived on our street and found out about it.

Had I been smarter I would never have been caught, but instead of turning the bottles in as I took them, I saved them in a fort I made in the rafters of the garage. I lined the bottles up in rows according to type, all the Coke on one side and the Crush on the other with everything else in between. When I had so many bottles they were pushing the limits of the fort, my mother noticed the gleaming lines of glass.

"What's up in your fort, Seth?"

"Just some old bottles."

"Looks like quite a collection of them. Where did you get so many?"

"Around."

"Where around?"

In the end she guessed the truth and had me line them up bottle by bottle on the garage floor.

"They're just bottles, Mother. You only get two cents for them."

"Son, my little brother and I found a candy bar when I was little. They only cost two cents then because it was the Depression. Hans was not old enough to know any better, so I hid the big part of the candy bar in the wrapper and broke off the little end so he would think I had given him half. He never knew I cheated him. I'm thirty-five now, and I still feel bad about that two-cent candy bar every time I visit him."

"You really did that?"

"I did, and I never told him."

"You should have."

"I'll tell you what I'll do. You take the bottles back, and I'll mail a candy bar to Uncle Hans."

"But I don't remember where I got them all."

"Load them all in boxes and pile them in your wagon. Knock on all the doors in the neighborhood and ask the people if they're missing some bottles."

I knocked on the first door and asked the question.

"I stole some bottles a few days ago. Were any of them yours?"

I got a puzzled look.

"I'm bringing them back so I won't feel bad about it when I'm thirty-five."

At every house it was the same. People took back what they thought was theirs, and when I was done I still had bottles left over.

It made me mad at my mother. I got home and crawled under the coffee table and wrote "Mother is mean" in black crayon. Mother always let us take out our anger that way. When she knew we were mad she would bring us the crayon, and we'd crawl under the table.

I felt bad about everything now, so I was anxious to get baptized and have those awful memories gone. Two of my friends were to be baptized with me. We talked about it after Sunday School.

"Is your dad going to come?"

"No, he lives in Salt Lake. I only see him during the summer."

"Who's going to baptize you, Seth?"

"Bert."

Bert was the best friend our family had. He was always doing things for us. He was short and stout with a large midsection that flowed over his belt. He laughed constantly, which jiggled his center violently. My sisters and I called our own stomachs "Berts," and one night we locked ourselves in the bathroom and tried to get them to shake like his.

Bert had a son who had just been made a priest. He would baptize me, and Bert would confirm me the next day.

We drove down to the old ward building on "F" Street together. Above the entrance to the chapel was a stained glass window of the First Vision. I tried hard to believe it really happened. I didn't know for sure, but I knew Mother knew, and that was enough, the bishop told me.

We went downstairs to the font, and I put on my white clothes. I sat down next to Bert's son and watched as my friend's fathers took them down into the water and baptized them.

I stepped into the water and heard my full name; then I felt myself going under the water. When I came up, I looked at my mother.

"I'm going to be good from now on, Mother, so I won't have to sit in your class."

She kissed me and handed me a towel.

I kept thinking that all the way home and right up until I went to sleep.

The next day was Fast Sunday and my confirmation. Normally it was the worst meeting of the month for me. I fasted the two meals for the first time in my life. I wasn't sure what it meant to be confirmed, but I knew it was important because it was done in front of the whole congregation. I sat next to my mother at the back of the chapel and waited for Bert to come in.

I had just sat through my first Sunday School class without making a sound or shooting rubber bands. The bishop started the meeting.

"We have three confirmations today. Would Patrick, David, and Seth please come to the front."

I watched my friend's fathers walk them down the aisle and sit with them on the front row.

"Go ahead," Mother whispered. "Bert will be here."

I walked down the aisle and joined my friends. First Patrick, then David stepped onto the stand and sat down.

"By the power of the Melchizedek Priesthood . . ." The words came slowly, and then my friends returned to their seats. I was alone on the front bench, and it seemed to stretch forever. I looked up at the bishop and his counselors who were talking quietly. The congregation was whispering behind me.

"Seth, come up and sit down in the chair."

The whole congregation was looking at me, turning their heads from time to time to study the back door. One of the counselors put his hand on my shoulder, guiding me into the chair, and turned me to face the back of the chapel.

"Seth, was Bert going to confirm you?"

I nodded. He looked up at the bishop, then went on.

"Bert isn't here today, Seth. Is there someone else you'd like to confirm you?"

"No."

"There must be someone."

I looked over the congregation trying to see my mother. All I could see were faces. Some of them were familiar, but I didn't know any names. I looked up at the three faces above me.

"You do it."

I put my head down and felt the weight of their hands. I wanted to listen for the voice Grandpa told me about and see if I could feel His smile, but I couldn't control my emotions. I was just grateful to put my head down. They finished and I returned to my mother's side. Bert walked in just as I was sitting down. I wasn't mad at him. I knew something had come up.

"I'm sorry, Seth," he whispered.

"It's all right. The bishop did it."

"I'll make it up to you," he said.

The resolve to be perfect waned with the coming weeks. Four years later when I finally graduated from Primary and Junior Sunday School, I had earned the nickname "Holy Terror of the Primary." The teachers celebrated their liberation with a victory party, and the whispers were so thick you could read them on the chapel walls.

Bert did make it up to me. He bought me a pair of Bantam chickens to raise.

"You'll need a place to keep them, Seth. Let's build a chicken coop."

He led me out behind the garage. I worked with him most of the day, and when dinner was ready I closed the door on my new chickens, knowing they were safe inside.

"Something depends on you for life now. You'll have to take care of them."

"I will, Bert. I'll be real good to them."

I spent some time every day inside the coop with the chickens. I watched them grow. I was the only boy in the neighborhood who had chickens. All my friends wanted to see them.

"This is called a coop. I helped build it."

They looked at me with wonder.

"I named them Joseph and Nina after my grandpa and grandma."

"Did you tell them?"

"I wrote to my grandpa, and he sent back a little note saying they were fitting names—especially Nina. He said it was about time I had my own Relief Society to look after."

I often thought about them during school and waited for the bell to ring so I could come home and let them out into the yard. Joseph always flew to the top of the wall and strutted back and forth, standing guard, while Nina pecked in the grass of the lawn. They would patiently follow me around the yard waiting for me to scare up an insect to eat.

I loved my chickens. They filled an emptiness I felt when I watched my friends play ball with their dads. Mother played ball with me too, but it felt funny to have her in the street with everyone watching. My friends' dads all watched the day she tried to teach me how to ride a bike. She couldn't run fast enough to catch me before I fell, so she pointed me to a thick section of grass next to the curb. I tried to get that far before I went down. It didn't work very well, though, and she finally gave the boy next door a dollar to run me up and down the street. I got teased about that, but about the chickens I was a miniature hero.

A few months later I came home for lunch to an empty house. Mother always came home from work to fix us lunch.

"Mother! Where are you?"

"Behind the garage. Come on out."

I ran to where she was stooped over in one corner of the coop.

"Come here, Seth."

There was eagerness in her voice. I stepped into the coop and kneeled down beside her. She reached under Nina and carefully lifted her into the air.

"Look at the nest, Seth. Count the eggs."

Six eggs were neatly arranged in the center of the nest.

"Don't touch them. We'll watch them hatch, and then you can give a baby chick to each of your friends."

She put the hen back on the nest and closed the coop door. Joseph was strutting back and forth on the wall.

"I wonder what the little chickens look like inside right now," she said.

"Maybe like a breakfast egg?"

"I don't know. Let's go find out."

She took me to the bookshelf and pulled out the Childcraft books. We spent the lunch hour looking at pictures of developing eggs.

She was always like that—so eager to teach. Maybe that's why she became a teacher after the divorce. She made me think teaching was the greatest thing a person could do.

There was no end to the marvels she led me to discover.

"Sit on the grass with me, Seth, and watch this wasp."

"What's he doing?"

"She. It's a female. She's digging a hole. Then she'll drag that cater-pillar into it and lay her eggs. When they hatch they will have some-thing to live on."

She brought silkworms home and placed them on a shelf in the kitchen.

"You'll have to gather mulberry leaves everyday. They eat raven-ously."

"Why not the leaves in the backyard?"

"They only eat mulberry leaves."

We watched them spin their cocoons and emerge days later as velvet white moths.

Once we went to the beach.

"See where the wave stops, Seth? Watch for the feelers. There. Now run and scoop up the sand."

"I can feel them tickling. They're trying to dig through my hands."

"Those are the sand crabs. Let the water wash the sand away and you can see them."

Through it all she taught me of a Heavenly Father who cared about every creature and provided for its needs. I learned to love Him because I loved the things He had created. Spiders, lizards, and hornytoads from the fields, frogs from the swamp, rats from the pet shop, and even an opossum all found acceptance in my mother's eyes. I loved life as she showed it to me, and loving helped satisfy my hunger.

The eggs finally hatched. Mother and I sat inside the coop and witnessed each baby chick peck its way to freedom.

"Five little Ninas," I said, "and one black Joseph. I'm going to give them to my friends."

"Not until they're big enough to leave the mother."

I don't know who left the coop door open. I blamed everyone else, but the chickens were my responsibility. I came home from school and saw the hole under the gate and rushed around the garage. The coop door was wide open, and dogs were everywhere. Two of them were fighting over the body of the hen. The chicks were gone.

I stared at the dogs for a few seconds. One of them was sitting just inside the coop door with his mouth open and his tongue hanging out. He was smiling. I forgot every fear I ever had of big dogs and tore into them with a fury. I grabbed a shovel that was leaning against the garage and drove the whole pack howling to the hole under the gate. They couldn't all fit at the same time so I beat each one as he struggled to get out and kept beating the empty hole when they were all gone.

I dropped the shovel and stared back at the coop, then walked over to the remains of the hen.

"Why did you do it? Why didn't you fly away?"

Something moved on the wall, something black. It was Joseph, unharmed, and strutting back and forth as he used to do. I walked over by the coop and stared.

"You shouldn't be alive, Joseph. How could you watch it? I hate you, Joseph. I hate you because you're still alive."

I screamed at him. I picked up a rock and threw it at him. He sat on the wall with his head cocked to one side. I threw another rock and knocked him off the wall. He squawked in pain and fright. I sat on the ground and watched him timidly approach me.

"I shouldn't be angry with you, Joseph. You didn't know any better. But I can't keep you. I can't love you anymore."

Mother tried to talk me out of it, but I couldn't find it in my heart to forgive him. We took Joseph to a farm outside of town, and I dismantled the chicken coop.

I hated those dogs, hated them with a vengeance that almost made me sick. I vowed through my hate to get even. I keep seeing the smiling face of the black dog sitting in the doorway of the coop. I searched the neighborhood until I found out where the black dog lived and turned all my hate to him. I talked to all my friends, and together we planned to kill the black dog.

I watched until only the little boy who owned the dog was home, then gathered my friends. We armed ourselves with rocks and sticks and went hunting for the dog. When we finally found him, we threw rocks at him and chased him all over the neighborhood. The boy who owned him was smaller than we were and could do nothing except run after us crying and screaming at his dog to run away.

"He killed my chickens, and I'm going to kill him."

We finally cornered the dog on his own front porch. He was too exhausted to run anymore, so he sat and whined. We gathered around him about six feet away and closed the circle. I had two big rocks in one hand and a stick in the other. The boys were waiting for me to throw the rocks because I made them promise I could get him first. I saw Nina with her outstretched wings trying to protect her chicks and raised my arm, oblivious to the screams of the little boy behind me, but I couldn't throw the rock. A voice I had never heard before was talking. The words formed inside me one by one.

Seth, it is wrong to kill.

"But he killed my chickens!" I thought I screamed it, but the other boys didn't look at me.

"Don't kill my dog! Please don't kill him!"

"He killed my chickens!"

The voice came back.

Look at the dog, Seth.

"He killed my chickens!" I screamed again. This time the boys looked at me.

Look at the dog.

I didn't want to look at him. I wanted to kill him. I was losing. I squeezed my eyes shut and saw the smiling face just inside the coop door.

"He killed my chickens! He killed my chickens! I'm going to get him!"

The voice sighed. I felt its shudder pass through my body. *Look at the dog!*

It was a command. I opened my eyes and saw the dog sitting in the corner. He was shaking all over now, howling. I could still hear the pleas of the little boy, who had now crumpled to the grass. I could understand his love, for I had known it too.

I dropped the rocks and walked away without explaining to my bewildered friends. They never asked me about it, and I never volunteered an answer. We just dropped the rocks and never spoke of the chickens or the dog again.

I went home and lay on my bed and shut my eyes.

"Grandpa, what does the voice feel like?"

"It makes you quiver inside, but not hard so it hurts—soft like aspen leaves trembling in the wind, like the sparrow's heart when you held her in your hand. And nothing else has any room inside you while it's speaking. Do you understand, Seth?"

"No, Grandpa. Are there words?"

"Only if there needs to be, but you'll understand without them, and you'll let it bend you like these carrot tops bend when the breeze blows over them."

5

Uncle Morgan

The summer after Uncle Jens died, Mother once again urged me to spend the summer at Uncle Morgan's ranch. It was a hard decision. I had to go alone on a bus to Elko. My sisters would go to Utah with Mother. I didn't want to miss gardening with my grandfather and the Relief Society "sisters." Then there was my father. The last three summers he had taken us to Lagoon. In the end, however, I boarded the bus for Elko.

The only contact I had with my father from then on was the monthly envelope he sent. It was always the same—three checks for twenty-five dollars each made out to my sisters and me. I would look at the scribbled signature at the bottom of his checks and wonder why he never sent a letter.

The ranch was a hundred miles from Elko. The last thirty miles covered the roughest suggestion of a road imaginable. The ranch was the last stop. From there you had to go on foot or horseback. It sat at the bottom of a long canyon. A river ran through the hay fields that lined the canyon bottom. Huge cliffs towered here and there over the river and fields. It was like retreating a hundred years into the past.

Uncle Morgan was the only man I knew who could do anything. Grandpa had limits, but not Uncle Morgan. He had lived his whole life in the confident spirit of the old frontier. He disdained modern methods of ranching, preferring horses to tractors, lanterns to electricity. He braided his own ropes from strips of cowhide soaked for days in the river. He refused to see a doctor unless my aunt forced him to, and he swore no pill ever made could cure arthritis as effectively as copper bracelets around the joints. He wore one on each wrist and ankle. They turned his skin a permanent green.

Every other man I knew towered above me—not Uncle Morgan. Even in the prime of his life he stretched to only five feet six inches, but fifty-five years of riding had bowed his legs and stolen two inches. An injury to his hip from a bull took another inch and left him with a permanent hobble. He was shorter than my aunt and said that he had married a taller girl to "improve the strain." It had worked—his four sons and two daughters were all taller than he was.

The only thing that stopped him from working on the ranch, which he loved with a passion, was sleep. He could fall asleep in any position within seconds, which he frequently did at inopportune moments.

His life was not organized like my grandfather's. Old bits of harness, bolts, broken wagon wheels, and rusty mower blades lay scattered behind every building and trailed off into the sagebrush. He threw nothing away, for sooner or later everything had a use. He could lay his hand on the slightest, twisted piece of metal at a moment's notice. The old-fashioned haying equipment was held together by his ingenious use of broken parts and his determination to make everything last one more year.

He was completely unaffected by pain, never cried, and laughed continuously from deep in his chest. His only weakness was ice cream. He could eat a half gallon at a sitting. He once ran five miles, his joints aching, and me trailing behind him, to save a half gallon of ice cream from melting in the August sun. We had run out of gas coming back from buying supplies. A half mile from the ranch he gave up. Dripping with melted ice cream, we sat down to drink the last of it.

My first week at the ranch, Uncle Morgan caught a badger that was killing chickens in the middle of the night. Before he could raise the .30-30, the badger bit his leg. He shot the badger with its teeth still in his leg, then pried the jaws loose with his fingers while he bit into an old leather strap. From that moment on, I was in total awe of him.

The first thing Uncle Morgan did when I returned that summer was to give me a horse of my own and teach me to ride. My horse was a little roan colt born that spring. He was going to break her for me so I could ride her the next summer. We put the horses on the top of the mountain above the ranch to feed. I often lay in the thick grass of the front lawn and gazed at the mountaintop through the Chinese elms that surrounded the ranch house and thought of my horse up there running through the sage. It was a good feeling.

Uncle Morgan insisted that I learn to ride well enough to keep up with him.

" Climb on this horse, Seth, and we'll go riding."

We were gone for hours before we turned our horses back to the ranch. When we got to within a mile of the house, my horse bolted and ran for the barn. I dropped both reins and grabbed the saddle horn, crying at the horse to stop and for my uncle to help me. The ground disappeared behind me like flowing water. I began to bounce around on the saddle. I heard my uncle's horse coming up fast behind me.

"Pick up the reins! Let go of the saddle horn and ride!"

"I can't let go! I'll fall off!"

He caught me just before I came to the bridge. He leaned out far from his horse, grabbed my reins, and pulled both horses to a stop. I scrambled off as fast as I could and sat down on a rock. He watched me for a few minutes, then handed me the reins of my horse.

"Here, get on. Let's go on home."

I looked at his outstretched hand as he leaned down from his horse. No force on earth was going to get me on the back of that horse again.

"I want to walk, Uncle Morgan. It's not far. I don't want to ride."

He didn't withdraw the offered reins. "Seth, get on your horse. No nephew of mine walks to the corral leading his horse because he's afraid to ride it."

I turned to pull myself into the saddle, but the memory of the flashing of ground disappearing behind me was still too strong. I didn't look at him.

"I'm afraid, Uncle Morgan."

"I'm afraid too, sometimes, but a man doesn't let that bother him."

The answer seemed impossible to believe.

"You hold the reins, Seth. You make him do what you want him to do. Now climb on your horse, and let's go home."

I looked over my shoulder up into his sunburnt face and the old work hat with the greasy sweatband. He smiled at me. I took the reins and climbed cautiously back into the saddle. He kicked his horse and galloped off toward the corral, leaving me alone in the road. My horse galloped after him, and panic gripped my stomach, but his words played back in my mind, and I jerked the reins with a suddenness that pulled the bit high in the horse's mouth. He stopped. "I hold the reins, and you do what I want you to do!" He turned his ears as if trying to understand, then we galloped off after my uncle.

My uncle made the boy in me seem far away. I would have done anything for him. He taught me things my mother could never teach. I sat on the riverbank and watched his fingers inch a worm up the hook.

"Now you try it. Bite the hook down into the center and slip it around the end. Now throw it there, by the ripples where the water's black."

He made me the official hay stacker and only grunted when I drove the pitchfork through his boot. "You're doing so good, Seth, I think I'll let you do it alone. I'm just getting in your way."

My first stack curved precariously to one side. The slant on the top wasn't right, and the corners were far from square. He combed the sides with his fork, then stood next to me with his arm around my shoulder. "That's a great stack."

"It doesn't look like the ones you make, Uncle Morgan."

"That's all right, Seth. It's a little different, but the water can run down the back side where you curved it."

I thought I was the greatest rancher in the world. The stack sat across the river from the ranch house. I stared at it when we ate our meals on the patio. It fell over later that summer.

"Craziest thing I've ever seen, Seth, that stack falling over like that. I didn't even hear the windstorm last night, did you?"

"I didn't hear anything."

"Must have been some storm to blow a whole stack over."

One day he told me to climb into his truck.

"How old are you now, Seth?"

"Almost ten."

"Well, that's old enough to learn how to drive on these roads. You can drive my truck. It's easier than the old Willys."

He opened my door, and I climbed into the cab. "I can't touch the pedals."

"Scoot up on the seat. We'll put this gas can behind you." He handed me the key. "Put it into the ignition. Put your foot on the clutch—the far pedal to the left—and turn the key." I felt the truck rumble as the engine turned over.

"Now give it a little gas."

We jerked forward for a few jarring feet and rolled to a stop.

"Try again, Seth. Sometimes these trucks do that. They're temperamental." We lurched forward another few feet, and the truck rolled to a stop. I looked at my uncle.

"Worked fine yesterday. I'd better check it."

He stepped out of the cab and lifted the hood, examining various parts. When he was done, he wiped the grease on his pants and climbed back into the cab.

"Now try it. I think I got it fixed. Lift your foot off the clutch a little more slowly, too."

This time we kept moving. I was in first gear and rolling forward faster and faster.

"Now shift it. Put your foot back on the clutch, take your foot off the gas, and move it into second, down there by your leg."

I tried to follow his instructions and was greeted with a terrible grinding sound.

"That's okay. The gears are always a little tight on a new truck. You have to grind them down a bit so they'll shift smoother."

He helped me find second, then third, and laughed at my excitement. We drove down the road to the other ranch and around the corner of the hill to the main bridge.

I hadn't looked at him for a while because I was so busy watching the road. The bridge was coming up ahead. It sat on a hairpin turn across the river. I was going too fast so I took my foot off the gas and turned to my uncle for instructions. He had too much confidence in me. He had gone to sleep.

"Uncle Morgan, wake up!"

His hat was laid down over his eyes to shield them from the Nevada sun. His head bobbed from side to side with the motion of the truck.

"Uncle Morgan! We're coming to the bridge. What do I do?"

The bridge leaped up the road at me. Something told me I would never wake him up in time. I glanced at the pedals below me. I knew the brake was there, but wasn't sure if you pushed the clutch at the same time. I reached across the cab to shake him. The truck swerved. I barely righted it in time to turn sharply onto the bridge. I hit a pedal and kept going. I looked down and realized I was furiously pushing the clutch. I switched to the brake and turned the wheel. We narrowly missed the center brace of the bridge. I tried to make the corner of the bridge back to the road, but was going too fast. I sideswiped a clump of willows and stopped suddenly with the help of a boulder. I almost threw my uncle through the windshield.

He woke up in a daze, looking around to see what had happened. I braced myself for his rebuke.

"I couldn't stop the truck, Uncle Morgan. The corner was too sharp."

He climbed out of the cab and walked around front to look at the damage. I followed him, knowing what would greet us when we rounded the front fender. He looked at the large fold in his truck and rubbed his hand across the crease. He looked back at me, then smiled.

"You've got to watch out for these boulders, Seth. They'll jump out and grab a truck every time. This same boulder tried to get me a couple of times already."

He turned me around and led me back to the cab.

"Climb back in. I guess I need to show you how to back it up."

I climbed back in and backed away from the rock, and we drove home. When we got back to the house, he sat down next to me on the front step.

"Feeling bad about the truck, Seth?"

"I'm sorry. My mother will pay for it."

"I've thought of another way you can make it up to me."

"How?"

"Catch me a snipe. They're little birds, but they're real tricky to catch, and I'm getting old."

He gave a shrill little whistle and then gently clucked in his throat. "Can you do that?"

I practiced for an hour until the sun finally went down. He led me to the barn and pulled an old gunny sack from the grain barrel. He lifted it to his face and smelled it. "This is a good one," he said. "It smells like grain. That drives the snipes wild."

When we were almost to the little clearing where the snipes gathered, he decided he would hunt with me. "I'll go back and get another sack."

He limped down the hill to the barn, returning a few minutes later. A piece of string hung limply through his teeth. "You need something to tie the top of the sack with."

He gave me one, too, and I hung it between my teeth. We sat back-to-back in the clearing, and he began to whistle.

"I can hear one coming, Seth."

"I can't hear anything."

He leaped into the air and tore the string from his mouth.

"I've got mine, Seth!" He started swinging a brown and red feathered bird around his head. "You swing them so they won't peck your hand!"

The bird was squawking and straining to get away. He pushed it into the gunny sack, tied it with the string, and held it up to my eyes. The sack bulged and jumped as the bird tried to fight its way out.

"Sit back down. The next one is yours."

He ran down the mountain and left me breathlessly excited in the darkness, whistling and clucking enough to attract every snipe in Nevada. It was over an hour before I got hoarse enough and cold enough to give up and come down the mountain. Uncle Morgan was sitting on the front step of the house.

"Back so soon?"

The string was still dangling from my mouth.

"I guess I'm not as good a clucker and whistler as you are."

"Do you want to see it before we pull the feathers off and let your aunt cook it?"

He reached behind the porch and brought out the tied gunny sack. The bottom of the sack came alive with motion.

"You have to be careful or they can get away." He untied the sack slowly. "Peek inside just for a second."

I could see the snipe's brown feathers in the reflected lantern light. Suddenly Uncle Morgan opened the sack wide and bumped the bottom with his knee. I spilled over backward. Everyone was laughing. I opened my eyes and saw a large hen scrambling down the dirt road to her nest. Uncle Morgan's laughter was contagious, and I forgot all about the creased fender. For a week after, he would whistle and cluck frequently and laugh under his breath, and I laughed with him.

There was always work to be done, hard work. When the job was too difficult and I began to give up or complain, he would stand up to the top of his shrunken height, puff out his chest, put a rough expression on his face, and say through his gritted teeth, "Seth, it's good for you! It makes you tough!" That was all it took to put the fire back into me. He was the toughest man in the world, a combination of Orrin Porter Rockwell and Samson rolled into one. I wanted to be like him, so I did anything he said.

"Grab that calf, Seth, and hold him down so I can brand him."

I sat in the manure of the corral bottom holding down calves bigger than I was, breathing in the smell of their burning hair.

"That smoke is good for you, Seth. Don't make faces at it. It makes you tough."

I'd breathe in the smoke deeply so my lungs would be tough, too. If the calves kicked and struggled to get free, he'd yell, "Bite his ear, Seth. Show him who's boss." And when I did it, he tilted his head back with laughter. "That's right. It's good for you. It makes you tough. I can see you getting tough right now." That was all it took. They were magic words. He enjoyed saying them, and I loved to hear him say them, because each time he repeated them I knew I was becoming more like him.

He taught me how to milk a cow, tighten a loose strand of barbed wire on a fence, find my way on the desert or in the canyons, and drive a team of horses hitched to a wagon or rake. More importantly, he taught me how to tell a story.

He was full of stories—more than Grandpa. The desert and valleys were haunted with old buildings, mines, broken pieces of arrowheads, and blue bottles. He knew a story about every one of them, from the deepest mine shaft to the smallest chip of blue glass.

We were haying one day on a field next to an old homestead. It was a haunting place filled with old memories. A black, rotting haystack surrounded by a weathered log corral dominated the main hayfield, which the sage was beginning to reclaim. Across the road and up a little hill was an old shack. Rusted beaver traps and a splintered washboard hung from nails in its walls. A rotted, corrugated tin roof absorbed the sunlight and wreathed the shack in heat. A little pathway of colored rocks led to the door. A No Trespassing sign hung precariously to one side.

My uncle could see I was fascinated with it. After lunch he came over to me and whispered mysteriously in my ear, "You'd better not go peeking in that shack, Seth. There's something inside that will scare you."

He walked off behind the old rotting haystack. I made sure he was out of sight, then started up the hill. I pushed the door open as carefully as I could, ready to run should anything leap out at me. The door scratched on its rusted hinges, slowly letting the sunlight reveal the floating motes of dust hanging in the air. Because of the slant of the building, the door slammed shut as soon as I pulled my hand away. I had to push hard just to get it open. As the door was opening I caught the white glimmer of bones. Just then my uncle's hand fell on my shoulder. I jumped back, almost knocking him down. He caught me as I fell, then whispered, "Did you see him?"

"I saw some bones."

"Go ahead and open the door. Since you're up here, you might as well see him."

My throat filled with dust. I pushed the door open. There on the floor of the shack, amidst the rags and old bits of glass, lay the half-decomposed carcass of an ancient bull. He was huge, the biggest bull I had ever seen. His head was propped up against one of the walls, leaning on the stub of a broken horn. The hide was stretched in pieces across the carcass, revealing the bowed rib cage. The remainder of a field mouse nest poked through the ribs. The skull was perfectly bare. It sat, tilted, staring at the doorway. The mouth was half open in a semi-smile. For weeks after, I woke up seeing that grinning face and the empty stare of those hollow eyes.

"See how he smiles at you?"

I nodded.

"Would you like to know what happened to that bull?" I nodded and sat down next to him. The door slammed securely in place.

"That bull was the biggest bull in the whole valley. Not another bull could challenge his territory, and he gathered himself quite a harem. He used to strut around in front of all the cows and calves, letting them know just how big and important he was, and no one, to my knowledge, wanted to argue with him. He wasn't afraid of a thing, and he liked to prove it. It was no surprise to anyone when he insisted on investigating this shack.

"He brought his cows over the ridge, then strutted down the hill, swinging his tail casually. The door was pulled shut like it is now, and he could see the No Trespassing sign on it, but of course he couldn't read, so he kept right on coming.

"He walked around it a few times, then stopped right in front of it and blew steam on it. Nothing happened. He turned to look at the cows, who were all standing on the top of the hill in suspenseful awe.

"He pushed the door with his head, and it swung open, but as you saw, the slant pulls the door shut, so it slammed closed almost immediately and bumped him on the nose. It gave him a few slivers, and that made him mad. He pushed the door again and stared into the opening, but the door closed on him.

"He was more curious now. He stepped into the doorway and let the door rest on his shoulder so he could look around it. Right away he could see nothing was behind the door. Yet, it was still pushing hard against his shoulder. It made him just a little nervous. He decided to return to his cows on the hill. But a fatal thought grabbed him as he was about to back out. He wondered if the cows would still think he was the bravest bull in the valley if he backed out of the shack. No, he'd better go all the way into the shack, turn around, and walk out like any respectable bull would do if he weren't afraid.

"And that's what got him, Seth, those cows on the hill. He pushed the door all the way open, but when he turned around to get out, the door slammed shut, and he was trapped."

My uncle stopped for a few seconds, crooked his finger in front of me, and shook it slowly and impressively.

"You know, Seth, all the bellowing, snorting, and charging, and all the crying of his cows couldn't open that door one crack. As the days passed, he got weaker and weaker until he lay down like you saw him and never got up. He starved to death, and his cows were taken into other harems by lesser bulls. In time he was forgotten."

He stood up and pushed the door open once again, watching it slam shut with the tilt of the building.

"Forgotten by everyone but you and me, Seth. We won't forget him. No sir, we won't forget him."

6

Slide Rock

I disobeyed my uncle only once that summer. We were just finishing branding for the day. The sage fire I loved to smell had been reduced to crumbling ashes, and my cousins were just finishing the final separation of heifers, steers, and bulls.

"Climb on your horse, Seth, and run those heifers and calves up to the gate and push them out onto the desert. We'll hold the steers and bulls here."

I scrambled up the fence, grabbed the reins of my horse, and swung into the saddle. I pushed the heifers out of the corral and drove them to the gate about three hundred yards up the hill. I opened the barbed wire gate without getting off. The cows stepped through and moved down the fence line to the desert. I turned around and was starting back down the hill when one of the bulls broke through the fence and lumbered up the hill. My uncle hollered up to me to head the bull. I started after him. A few moments later I heard my uncle change his instructions.

"Just stay at the gate. I'll send the boys after him."

I turned and watched my cousins urging their horses out of the corral. I carried on a one-sided competition with my cousins. I was determined to be as good as they were at ranching and win a share of their father's acceptance. Now they were being sent to do the job. I watched them sweep through the gate, at one with the horses they rode.

"I can stop the bull," I said to myself, and kicked my horse down the hill. My uncle saw me moving and yelled a little louder.

"No, Seth. Stay where you are! The boys will get the bull. Don't come down the hill!"

I reined to a stop. The habit of obedience was hard to break. I should have stayed, but I pictured myself driving the bull back to the corral without the help of my cousins. I kicked my horse again and tore down the hill, whipping her into a full gallop. The wind rushed by me, filling my head with the smell of sage and cattle. I wasn't afraid anymore. I controlled the horse just as he had taught me.

Oblivious to anything around me, I closed in on the bull. My uncle stood at the bottom of the hill yelling and waving his arms. He climbed the fence, took his hat off, and waved it back and forth in a last appeal to stop me.

My cousins reined to a stop. The next thing I knew the horse was out from under me, and I was pitched through the air over her head. In a split second everything became crystal clear—my uncle waving his arms, his unusual frenzied shouts, and my cousins' abrupt stop. Hidden from above by the sagebrush, the hill took a sharp drop. I didn't see it until it was too late. No mare in the world could have kept her footing.

I was thrown clear of the saddle, then jerked backward as my foot, now tangled in the stirrup, pulled me back to straddle the mare's neck. Then we rolled. She pushed me into the dirt, ground my arms into the sage, and crushed my legs against the saddle horn. I arched over her back and was slammed into the ground again. Four times she rolled. Each time I was on top, I tried to free my foot. When she finally stopped, I was pinned underneath, and none of my protests could move her. I fought the dizzying blackness that waved over me. A boy passed out, not a man. Panic gripped me as I thought of the horse. What if she'd broken her leg, and we had to shoot her? She lay in the sage breathing heavily, letting her weight settle down on me.

From my position I could see the corral. My uncle moved up the hill toward me. He ran through the sagebrush, pushing bent legs forward. Slivers of pain shot up my leg into my back.

"I'm a fool," I muttered. "I've disappointed him. Now he's running up the hill to pick up the pieces."

He was out of breath when he finally reached me.

"I'm sorry, Uncle Morgan. Did I break her leg?"

He pulled the mare's head up, and when she still wouldn't move, he kicked her. She stood up immediately, taking me with her. I hung upside down from the stirrup. He untangled my foot and set me on the ground, then began poking me to be sure nothing was broken.

"I didn't see the drop."

"You're not hurt, are you? Nothing's broken?"

I looked into his face and read something there I had never seen in a man's face before.

"You're worried about me, not the horse?"

"Of course. That was a bad fall."

He helped me to my feet and walked down the slope with me. I hurt all over but wouldn't admit it.

"Uncle Morgan, I'm sorry I didn't listen to you. I wanted to stop the bull. I didn't want to wait for him at the gate."

He laid his hand roughly on my shoulder. The copper bracelets were warm against my neck.

"Why didn't you listen to me? Couldn't you hear me?"

I wanted to lie, but I couldn't, not to him. We walked a few more steps in silence.

"I could hear you."

"Then why did you come down the hill?"

"I wanted to show you I could ride as well as everyone else."

"Is it that important?"

"Yes."

He laughed from deep in his throat, not mockingly, but with delight.

"Well, we'll teach you to ride that well if you want to. I guess to be tough, you have to let a horse roll on you a few times."

We reached the corral, and he passed me the burlap-covered jug we used as a canteen. I lifted the jug and drank, letting the water spill down my chin and shirt, making little clean rivers through the dust on my clothes and skin.

"I'm going to tell you something, Seth, that I've tried to teach my own sons. Sometimes people can see things that will hurt you. They try to warn you, and if you keep on riding, if you don't listen to them, then you're going to get hurt, and you'll have no one to blame but yourself. That's true of more things than ranching, Seth. Do you understand what I'm trying to say to you?"

I wasn't sure I understood. He sounded like a teacher instead of an uncle, but if he said it, I knew it must be true.

"Uncle Morgan, I won't do it again."

"Do what, Seth?"

"Not listen to you."

He gazed up the hill to where the sage was broken and tangled by my fall and then beyond to the open gate.

"No," he whispered, "no, I don't suppose you will."

From that time on I knew I didn't have to prove anything to him.

As summer drew to a close, we went to the top of the mountain to bring the saddle horses down and check on the colts, my colt with them. We labored up the trail to the top of the cliffs where the mountain leveled off to form a natural bowl. The horses were grazing across the plateau when we finished our climb. I looked for my little colt. She was running next to her mother in the middle of the herd. The rest of the horses saw us approach and ran. We tried to get around them and head them back down the trail. They galloped across the mountainside, picking their way through boulders and slide rock. My colt threw her head high with a wild abandon of freedom that sent lightning down my back.

The herd slowed down. They had reached a stretch of very small slide rock and were inching their way across on a thin deer trail. Two of my cousins were carefully walking across the slide rock above the horses, trying to get around them and turn them back.

Everything happened so fast after that, it's hard to keep the events straight in my mind. Something spooked my colt. She jumped into the slide rock and went down. The rocks started moving, sucking her toward the cliff's edge. I jumped off my horse and ran, stumbling over boulders, falling down. Her feet were caught fast. More and more rocks tumbled down, taking her faster and faster down the slope. Then I was in the slide rock too, pushing with my knees to reach her.

"Uncle Morgan! I can't reach her. I can't stop her. She's going over the cliff!"

You can't save her, Seth! Stop moving!"

"I've got to stop her!"

"You're caught in the rocks! Stop moving!"

His warning brought me back to my own situation. The cliff's edge was only thirty yards below me.

"Spread your legs and dig in with your elbows!"

I slowed down, but not completely.

"Harder! Dig your elbows into the rock!"

I came slowly to a stop, turned my head to the cliff's edge, and watched in desperation as the slide carried my colt over the cliff and dropped her three hundred feet below.

I worked my way out of the rock and crawled to the edge of the cliff. By lying down I could peer over the drop. The rocks were still pouring over the top where the colt went over. I could see her far below me, half buried in rocks. She was still moving. I half slid, half stumbled down the mountainside, begging that she would be all right, begging for a miracle that would take the fear away. Someone was climbing down after me.

"Don't go down, Seth!"

"She's still alive!"

I looked over my shoulder. I saw him fall on his bad leg, right himself, and continue down the slope.

"She's dead. Don't go down!"

"I saw her moving!"

I reached her a few seconds before he caught up with me. She was lying on her side, her stomach rising and falling, a rasping escaping from her throat. I knelt down and placed my hand on her heaving sides. She struggled to get up, her eyes wide with fear, then lay back down on the rocks. My uncle knelt beside me and lifted my hand from her side.

"Her windpipe is broken. She'll never live."

I knelt in the silence, staring down at the broken windpipe pushing through her neck. The tears came in a rush, shaking my body.

"She's in pain. We can't let her stay in pain."

"I don't want her to be in pain, Uncle Morgan."

"You climb back up to your horse. I'll be right up."

He turned me around and walked part of the way up the hill with me.

"They always die, don't they?"

"You can't change that, Seth. No one can change that. What's important is that she lived, if even for a short time."

I felt his hand leave my shoulder, knowing he was going back down to the colt. I could still hear her labored breathing rasping through the broken windpipe. I didn't turn around, but I could see it all in my mind—my uncle's hands curling around the rock and lifting it high in the air, the short grunt as he threw his whole force into its descent, the soft thud as it struck the colt's head. Then there was silence. I looked at my four cousins standing on the top of the cliff and heard the trickle of rocks still sliding over its edge.

I didn't talk to anybody that afternoon but went down to the bunkhouse and lay on my bed. I heard the footsteps on the stone walkway just outside the door and knew by their uneven tread that they belonged to my uncle. He came in and sat down next to me. Neither one of us spoke. He drew little circles with his worn boots in the dust of the bunkhouse floor as he turned his hat around and around in his fingers.

"You'll be going home soon, Seth."

"Next week."

"We've been glad to have you here this summer. You've been a lot of help to us."

I stared at a strip of flypaper hanging in the corner of the room. It hadn't been changed for months and was covered with black gnats.

"Will you come back next summer?"

"If my mother will let me."

"Well, I guess she'll let you. Now come with me. I want to show you something."

He led me out of the bunkhouse and down across the flat by the house. We crossed the front lawn and balanced our way across the metal flume that channeled the river water onto the lawn. He pointed to a little hill across the fields that jutted out from the main valley floor.

"On the top of that little rise over there is a pile of bones. Whenever I ride that way I take a little detour to see them. I didn't at first, but I have recently. They belong to an old horse I used to ride, a little mustang named Lightning."

He reached down and grabbed a handful of river sand, letting it sift slowly through his fingers.

"I rode him for fifteen years. He was small but always held his own with the other horses. I always thought he was like me, small and tough—like you're becoming. I kept him around even when he was too old to be of any use. One day he walked up the side of that hill, lay down, and died. I was mowing that day. As I made the rounds, I could see him standing on the top of the hill with his nose in the wind. When I made the last round, he was gone. I knew he was dead. I didn't go up there for the longest time. Then one day, almost by chance, I rode toward the spot he died on. His bones were there, bleached white and scattered by animals. Seeing them made me feel bad that he was dead, but I thought back on all the times he carried me and was glad for the fifteen years I spent on his back. Now I ride by and think of the fifteen years.

"Don't go hard inside, Seth. Don't let the best part of you drop over the cliff after your colt. It does no good to think of the bad times, the pains and the hurts. They come and go. We learn from them and keep living. And when our own time comes, we thank God for the things we've learned. You come back next summer, and we'll give you another horse, one already broken so you can start riding him as soon as you get here."

He left me sitting on the flume looking at the spot he had pointed out. It took me awhile to find the bones, but they were there, just as he said. The sun had bleached them white, making them stand out against the red earth. Higher up the mountain the buzzards were already circling. I wondered how long it would be before another pile of bones bleached white in the sun. Sadness came with the thought, but with it came also a feeling of warmth. I shared something with my uncle, something private. I knew that as long as the sun rose over the valley lighting two small heaps of whitened bones, I would be a part of my uncle and he would be a part of me.

7

More Than a Presence

When I returned to California, Uncle Morgan became a memory, and memories grow. I no longer looked at the signature on the bottom of the monthly check. School was starting, and I was going into the fifth grade. It was a stepping-stone year. There were the evenings at home with Mother as she told us stories of her youth, and, of course, there was Grandpa. Mother invited my grandparents to spend the winter and early spring months in California with us. Every day he was there with knife-sharpened pencils in his pockets and the worn leather Bible on his knee.

"Grandpa, why do you read the scriptures all the time?"

"Close your eyes, Seth."

"Why?"

"I want you to see something."

"How can I see something with my eyes closed?"

I closed my eyes and heard the rustle of dragonfly wings coming from his knee.

"What do you see?"

"Nothing. My eyes are closed."

He turned the pages again and began to read.

"'And there went out a champion out of the camp of the Philistines, named Goliath. . . . He had an helmet of brass upon his head, and he was armed with a coat of mail. . . . He had greaves of brass upon his legs, and a target of brass between his shoulders. And the staff of his spear was like a weaver's beam.'

"Now, Seth, what do you see?"

"A giant."

"How tall is he?"

"Taller than you."

"Look again. How much taller?"

"With me standing on your shoulders."

"What color is his armor?"

"I don't know."

"Look and see."

"Black."

"Black?"

"Black and shiny with lots of leather straps."

"How long is his spear?"

"From here to the window."

"He's standing at the bottom of a valley. There are armies on both hills. A few yards ahead of him is a stream. Can you see the stream?

"Yes."

"'And he stood and cried unto the armies of Israel . . . choose you a man for you, and let him come down to me. . . . I defy the armies of Israel this day: give me a man, that we might fight together.' What expression is on his face, Seth?"

"He's frowning and angry. He's shaking his spear at them."

"That's good. Keep your eyes closed."

"'And David rose up early in the morning, . . . and he came to the trench. . . . And David spake to the men that stood by him, saying, . . . Who is this . . . Philistine, that he should defy the armies of the living God?' Can you see David now?"

I nodded.

"How big is he?"

"As big as Becky."

"What's he wearing?"

"A sheepskin."

"No armor?"

"Just a skin."

Grandpa read, and I, with my eyes closed, listened and saw the scriptures come to life in my head. After David had slain Goliath, Grandpa asked, "How do you feel, Seth, right now, inside?"

"Different."

"How different?"

"Like someone is watching me."

"Good, Seth, Someone is watching you. That's why I read the scriptures. They remind me that someone is watching."

Every Wednesday night, we had an early supper and moved into the front room. Mother or Grandpa pulled down the scriptures and read. I crawled underneath the lamp table and used the pattern on its wooden underside to imagine scenes described by my mother and Grandpa. The legs of the table helped to black out the world and focus my attention. When the preaching and speeches came, I couldn't create the scenes and my mind wandered, but when they told the stories, I could see them—Daniel and Elijah, the four sons of Mosiah, Samuel the Lamanite hurling challenges from the walls of Zarahemla.

My sisters helped me gather all the old Christmas trees from the curbs and haul them into the backyard. We had more than fifty. I played lost in the wilderness and broke my bow like Nephi. The trees didn't last too long, however, and by February, when we couldn't see the lawn for brown needles, the trees went into the incinerator. They made a lovely blaze, and for a few minutes, Nebuchadnezzar couldn't make me bow down either.

I was lying under the lamp table one night listening to Grandpa tell about the brother of Jared and prayer. When he gave the family prayer, he would wait a long time before talking. His words always came slowly, with Danish phrases interspersed. I always listened to see what he would say about me, because we were all included by name in his prayers.

When he finished with the brother of Jared and I could see the rocks light up in my mind, he turned to my mother.

"Tell them the black dog story. They've heard enough stories from the scriptures."

Mother's stories gave me a sense of beginning. I had no beginning without them; my life started in the middle chapters. Only my parents and grandparents knew the title page.

"When I was young I used to walk past a yard where a large black dog lived."

I closed my eyes and created the scene.

"I dreaded having to walk past his house because he always ran after me. Most of the time I walked home from school with my brother. We crept as close to the house as we could and then ran past the front yard to a fence. Every day we ran, and every day the dog chased us. If we got over the fence, we were safe.

"One day I was walking home alone when he finally caught me. I didn't get started right, and the dog cut me off. I stood frozen to the sidewalk, watching him growling and charging. When he got right up to me, I couldn't think of anything to do but scream. I yelled as loud as I could, 'Heavenly Father, help me!' As the dog was jumping on me, he flipped right over on his back, doing a complete circle in the air. Someone's hand had caught him under the chin and whirled him backward. He was so shaken up that he ran back to the porch and let me go."

She finished speaking. I could still see the scene on the underside of the lamp table.

"Tell us another story about when you were little," I asked.

"Your grandfather's life is more interesting than mine. We'll have him tell one."

Grandpa told a story from Denmark, but I loved Mother's best. I had her tell it to me over and over again until her picture became more real to me than the scriptures.

"Don't you have any other stories like the black dog?"

"Not many that I could tell you, Seth, but Grandpa has hundreds."

On the morning of my tenth birthday I found a flat, plainly wrapped package next to my breakfast. We always ate breakfast before we were allowed to open our presents; it was torture, but somehow I choked down a bowl of cornflakes. I took the package from the table and untied the ribbon. I opened it slowly, removing the tape without tearing the paper. A green felt-covered binding appeared. On the front, spelled out in gold trim, were the words "My Life." I opened the first page and read the beginning sentence: "I was born in Copenhagen, Denmark, December 18, 1881."

"These are the stories your Grandpa's told you, Seth, and a lot you've never heard."

Grandpa sat at the end of the table adjusting his suspenders and cleaning his glasses. I looked up to thank him.

"I'm just an old Dane, Seth, but your mother thought you should have those stories. Don't let them become more important to you than the scriptures."

I turned the pages until I came to the end. On the second to the last page a new title appeared, "A Testimony to My Son." There were two stories on those pages. The first was the story of my mother's conversion; the second was the black dog story.

I took the book to school with me and read it during recess. I was afraid to let my friends see it. I didn't want them to know how much it meant to me. They found out and thought it was great. The next few days I read them all of Grandpa's stories, and at night I re-read them to my sisters, but I never read anyone else the last two. I couldn't.

At night I lay in bed and created the stories in my mind as Grandpa had taught me. One night a question appeared with the spinning black dog.

"Why did my father have to teach you about God and prayer when you learned it already by being saved from the dog? Why didn't you remember the story all your life?"

"Sometimes our memory keeps what our mind forgets. We choose to forget certain things that have happened to us because to think about them will make demands on us we don't want to fulfill. We don't really forget them—we just keep covering them up, hoping they will go away and leave us alone."

"You don't want me to ask about those things, do you?"

"No, Seth, some things are best forgotten."

"Like the things my father did?"

"Yes. We'll leave those things forgotten."

I thought about her words for a long time, asking her to repeat them when I couldn't remember them exactly. I thought of Uncle Jens. Maybe he had no spiraling dog in his own life, and he had started drinking. Maybe the same thing was true of my father, and that's why he didn't live with us anymore. So I asked her.

"Did anything like the dog ever happen to my father?"

She told me stories of the war. He'd had many things like the dog in his life. That made me worry even more.

"Why is he covering up all those things? What would he have to do if he remembered them?"

"I can't answer all those questions, Seth. Other things became more important to him, but I'm sure he still remembers them."

"They weren't enough?"

I went into my sister's room.

"Jan, will God give you a miracle if you ask Him for one?"

"I don't think so. You have to be a prophet."

"But Mother had one with the dog."

"That was different."

"I want a miracle to happen to me like Mother's and the stories in the scriptures."

"You won't get one."

"I want it to be a big one so I won't end up like Uncle Jens or our father or stay away from the Church and do some things like Mother did."

"What do they have to do with miracles?"

"Maybe if you have a big enough miracle, you won't drink or run away from your family. You'll be good because you'll always remember the miracle."

"You can be good without one, too."

"Grandpa had lots. I read them in my book, and he's good now. I think I've had some too."

"When?"

"At the ranch. I almost drove the truck off the bridge."

"That wasn't a miracle."

"The horse rolled on me and I wasn't even hurt, and I could have fallen off the cliff when my colt got caught in the slide rock."

"I don't think those are miracles, Seth, but you don't need one to be good. You're good now."

"Not really. I do bad things."

"Like what?"

"At church. I don't listen, and I get in trouble at school."

"Everybody does those things. You're a good boy, and you don't need a miracle."

In spite of that I still worried. Then my chance came. I was walking home from the store when a large German shepherd came running across the street after me. It was playing with some children on the front lawn and thought I was one of them. I panicked and turned my back to run. The dog sensed my fear and chased me. I screamed, "Help!" The dog jumped on my shoulders and brought me down in the street, biting my back and neck.

"Somebody help me, please!"

The dog's owner finally pulled the dog off.

"Are you all right, kid?"

I tried not to cry.

"He was only playing with you, but you got scared and ran. He didn't mean to hurt you."

I sensed the fear in his own voice.

"Why did you run?"

I looked at the dog sitting on the ground with his tongue hanging out.

I asked for help, just like my mother. It was a dog and everything. Why didn't He come?

"Kid, are you okay? How come you won't say anything?"

I tried to stand up. "I want to go home."

"Sure, kid. Let me help you. I'll take you in my car."

He turned to get in his car, but I left without him. I could see Mother's black dog flipping through the air, but now the German shepherd kept pushing the memory out. I ran to my house, then remembered that only Grandpa was home. I didn't know if he knew how to fix dog bites. I rang the doorbell several times before my grandfather opened it and let me in.

"Grandpa! I got bit by a big dog!"

He cleaned the wounds with a warm washcloth, one by one, talking to me as he dipped the cloth into the sink.

"How did it happen?"

"I was just walking home from the store. He chased me and knocked me down."

"Well, you're bit pretty bad, but I think you'll live."

"Grandpa? It didn't work."

"What didn't work?"

"I asked for help and nothing happened. I got bit anyway."

He stopped cleaning my back and began to dry it with a towel. He always took a long time to answer important questions.

"You asked your Heavenly Father to help you?"

"When I saw the dog coming, I yelled, 'Help me,' just like Mother."

"Who did you want to help you, Seth? Anyone or your Father in Heaven?"

"Does it matter?"

"It might."

I thought about his question for a moment. "I guess anyone."

He pulled a clean shirt carefully over my head.

"When I was nine, Seth, I ran errands for a fellow who made little wooden shoes. One day I was in the store in front of his house, and his wife came running in on fire. Something had happened to a gas stove that they cooked on. I took off my big leather apron and tried to wrap it around her, but I was too little, and she kept running around the room screaming for help. She was badly burned and had to be hospitalized. I thought about her for a long time because she was such a religious person that it didn't seem right she should get burned. I asked my father why God let it happen to her. He said, 'God can't stop everything bad.' I asked him then, 'Why didn't God help her before she got burned so badly?' Without really thinking he said, 'Because she didn't ask Him.'

I'm not saying your Father in Heaven won't help you unless you ask Him, but I think He likes to be asked. What do you think?"

"I think He likes to be asked too. I wish I had asked Him."

"Why?"

"Because then I would have a miracle like my mother to keep me good."

"Do you need a miracle to keep you good, Seth?"

I thought of Uncle Jens. Maybe Grandpa didn't think you needed a miracle to be good, but I knew I had to have one.

All the boys had rats for pets that spring. The demand was so great that the pet stores began to raise them to keep up with the need. I persuaded my mother to let me have some rats. I bought two for fifty cents each, a male and a female. The female was black and white, the envy of my friends.

Within days the rats became my best friends. I tried to sneak them to school with me, hiding them in the folds of my shirt next to my skin, but they tickled and I laughed. After the traditional wait in the principal's office, I took them home.

They sat on my shoulder wherever I took them. They rode with me to the pet shop for the sunflower seeds they devoured by the pound and to the grocery store to pick up old lettuce leaves. I let them run up my T-shirt, and they tickled me with their fur as they turned around inside to come out again.

I was playing with them on the front lawn one day when I noticed that the female was missing. I turned to look in the grass behind me. I couldn't see her anywhere. I rolled over to get a better look—maybe she had run into the ivy—when I felt a small nudge like a half-cupped hand under my hip. It gave as I rolled.

I knew what had happened. I turned over and saw her crushed into the grass, jerking uncontrollably. "I'm sorry," I cried. I scooped her up as carefully as I could, cradling her in my cupped hands, and ran inside to my mother.

By the time I reached the kitchen, the jerking had stopped. Her head was twisted grotesquely to one side, and her feet were pushed out from under her in the opposite direction.

"Mother! Look what I did. Can you help her? Or will she die?"

I could read the concern in my mother's eyes the minute she turned to look, and the helplessness.

"What happened, Seth?"

"I didn't mean to do it. It was an accident. I rolled on her while I was playing on the front lawn." I cried, not even trying to hold back the tears.

"There's nothing I can do."

She said it with a finality I refused to accept. I stood there staring at her unbelievingly.

"We'll go down to the pet shop right now, and you can pick out a new rat, any one you want, and I'll buy it for you."

"I don't want a new rat. I want this one." I still stared at her, expecting what no child has a right to expect.

"We'll have Grandpa build a little coffin for her, and you can bury her in the flower beds, and we'll have a funeral. Then we'll go down to the pet shop, and you can have any pet in the store."

"I don't want a coffin. I want my rat to be all right."

"I can't fix your rat. If I could I would do it, but I can't."

"Grandpa?"

I held the broken body up to show him. He picked up the rat gently and held her in the palm of his hand, her tail hanging limply between his fingers. He stroked the fur.

"Your mother's right, Seth. She's going to die."

I knew they were right. I couldn't argue with them both. Then it came—the whisper of promise.

"I'll ask Heavenly Father to fix my rat."

They looked at one another before either of them spoke. My mother broke the silence.

"Sometimes Heavenly Father doesn't give us everything we want."

I remembered the dog on my back, but shook off the doubt, knowing I had done it wrong that time.

"You told me He would answer prayers like He did when the black dog chased you, like He did in the scriptures and Grandpa's book."

"He does answer our prayers, Seth, but this is a little different."

"Why is it different?"

She waited for what seemed minutes. "I guess it isn't different. If you want to ask Him, you go ask Him."

"He'll have to learn."

I faced my grandfather. "You don't believe He will do it, do you, Grandpa, because she's just a rat."

My mother spoke. "Grandpa doesn't know. I didn't know when the black dog chased me. He doesn't want you to be disappointed."

My grandfather stroked the rat's fur, then placed her into my hands. "Don't you worry about what your grandpa thinks. You go ask your Father in Heaven. Kneel alone in your room and think in your mind that all God's creatures have a place in His heart, even the sparrows. Nothing's impossible. If the rat dies, it will be because Father in Heaven wants her to die; but don't you think about your grandpa."

I walked down the hall and into my room. I closed the door and laid my rat down on the black and brown striped bedspread. She was very still now, and I was afraid she had already died. But even if she had, Grandfather had assured me that nothing was impossible if only I could believe.

And I did believe, with a faith that was given as a gift for this one moment, one I received without words, through an impression, as Grandpa had once said I would.

Seth, this is a foundation. I give this freely with a love that will transcend all doubt. I give it to fulfill the prayer that has always been in the heart of your mother. I give it because a boy who now kneels believes his grandfather, believes that all creatures have a place in my heart. I give it because you ask in humility—not for the miracle, but for a deeper need.

I could not say much as I knelt, but it didn't matter. He knew and understood.

"Father. Please."

That was all. Then I became afraid. I thought of the dog sitting on my back. I lifted my head the tiniest bit to make it level with the crippled, motionless body on my bed. My heart sank. She was the same. Her head still bent to the side, her feet were still broken beneath her. But as I watched, she began to tremble. I felt His presence everywhere. I watched the broken body, watched as her head returned to its normal position and her whiskers moved, watched the broken feet gather beneath her to stand firm on the bedspread. She rose on her hind feet and smelled the air. I ran to my shelf and brought a sunflower seed. She reached for the morsel and tucked it into her cheek the way I had seen her do a hundred times before. I opened the door of my bedroom where my mother and grandfather were waiting.

"Look!" I unfolded my hands so they could see.

I could still feel His presence as Grandpa held the rat up to his eyes and my mother's filled with tears.

PART 2

Teaching Years

And though the Lord give you
The bread of adversity,
And the water of affliction,
Yet shall not thy teachers
Be removed into a corner
Any more.

But thine eyes shall see
Thy teachers:
And thine ears shall hear
A word behind thee,
Saying,
This is the way,
Walk ye in it,
When ye turn to the right hand,
And when ye turn to the left.

Isaiah 30:20-21

8

The First Goliath

On my twelfth birthday, my grandfather came from Utah to ordain me a deacon.

"Now you have the priesthood," he prayed, "and though you may receive high honors and great positions later in life, you will never walk taller or with more dignity than you do this day. The priesthood is a noble thing, Seth. It takes a noble man to bear it. Today when you stand at the sacrament table, you stand with Christ, for you bear more than His name now. People will watch you, Seth. They will watch to see if the priesthood makes any difference."

A week later I received my patriarchal blessing. One sentence, my mother told me, was the secret of life, and I should repeat it every morning before I went out the door. So I memorized it and tried to comprehend all that it meant: "Keep thyself clean and pure from the sins of this generation . . ."

I was beginning to see the walls that sin erected, walls built to shut out the truth because it hurt too much to face it, to admit it. I began to see the veiled truths brooding behind my own father's wall, and the old question, dormant for so many years, returned, because I could no longer ignore it. And I feared.

". . . and thou shalt walk without fear . . ."

I was so haunted by fears during those years. They came when other boys my age grew taller and stronger while I stopped growing. They came when I became the brunt of practical jokes and derision from the "hoods." They came with a startling rapidity that day I entered the restroom in high school and saw the polished steel blade through the clouds of cigarette smoke. They came with the war, with the draft, and with the memory of my Uncle Jens.

". . . and present unto thy companions and those who cross thy path an influence and light, that they might be led by thee from the ways of error unto the will and purposes of the Eternal Father."

Had I but known the light, perhaps it could have been different. If life's lessons could be remembered sooner, we could perform such miracles. I did not know then the power that made Him what He was. I know He tried to teach it to me. I should have discovered it so much sooner, but I did not, and an eternity of regret will never change those years. And would I change them? They were too valuable, too critical. They were the teaching years.

I met Phil after Christmas vacation. Everyone wanted to be his best friend, yet he chose me as soon as he moved into our school. Phil's enthusiasm was effervescent. He wore bright shirts that pulled your eyes out. He spoke faster than anyone, lining up his words like dominoes and then sending them spilling out in sentences where every word began before the last one ended.

I loved baseball because he loved it. I wanted to be as good as he was so I could raise myself above his sometimes condescending manner. Phil pushed me to practice hours longer than my initial interest commanded. I gained a self-confidence that came from being able to do something better than others. I spent hours imitating a basket style of catching. I even watched Willie Mays on television. I was chosen for a school team and played centerfield. We won the championship that year largely due to Phil's ability and an eighth inning double that I hit during the last game.

When summer came Phil urged me to stay home from the ranch so I could improve my hitting and learn to play first base. He wanted to pitch in Little League and hoped I would be his first baseman. We both had Little League dust in our eyes. When the time came, I almost did stay home, but Uncle Morgan's voice called more loudly, and I went to Nevada. Before I left, Phil gave me a first baseman's glove and a baseball.

On my way to the ranch I fingered the tight stitching on the cover of the ball, a resolve growing within me. Ever since that time with my rat, I had begun to see Him as my closest friend. I found myself discussing things with Him, things I would have felt foolish telling anyone else. As I grew older I talked with Him more and more, so now I began to plead, burying my face in the glove so the other passengers on the bus wouldn't hear me. "Let me be good. Let me hit this ball farther than any other player in the Little League."

Uncle Morgan gave me a new horse my first day there, but when we weren't working I wanted to play baseball. I forced my reluctant cousins to catch flyballs. I wondered if I had made the right choice in coming to the ranch. Phil was home practicing every day. I could see him in front of his garage firing his baseball at the circle he chalked there the day he told me he was trying out for pitcher. Maybe I should go home.

Uncle Morgan came around the barn. "Why don't you let me have a whack at that new ball of yours, Seth?"

He struck out twice, then we quit. I could do something better than he could, and I felt uncomfortable. Finally, I had my Aunt Pearl put me on the bus for Utah.

I spent a week at my grandparents' house constantly throwing the ball against the garage wall. I hadn't been out to the garden with Grandpa since I arrived. I felt a little guilty but not enough to choke out the resolve that was growing stronger every day. One day my grandfather walked past me carrying a bushel basket full of grass clippings. He dumped them on the compost pile, then watched me furiously hurling the ball at the garage. I could feel his eyes within the gold wire rims of his glasses following my every move. He came up to me and took his glasses off, polishing them with the tail of his shirt.

"You're getting pretty good with that baseball, Seth."

"My friend Phil and I are going out for a Little League team. He gave me this glove."

Grandfather grunted, unimpressed, and turned to examine the side of the garage. I grew nervous in that silence, wanting him to speak, to say something that showed he approved.

"Did you ever play baseball, Grandpa?"

"We didn't have it in Denmark."

"It's a good game."

"But a game. Are you still reading, Seth? I haven't seen you read since you came from the ranch." He sounded different, almost annoyed.

"I haven't had much time, Grandpa."

"Because of your practicing?"

"I guess. I enjoy it. I want to be good."

"Is this a Goliath, Seth?"

"Goliath?"

"Nothing. If you're going to be good at something, you'll need to practice."

He mumbled something in Danish as he shuffled into the house. I knew he was still watching me through the window with his hands folded solemnly behind his back.

"He doesn't understand. He doesn't understand how important it is to me because he has had to work all his life."

I fired the ball at the garage wall, scooping it into my glove as it shot back at me. I threw it all afternoon, but something was wrong. A black Goliath kept appearing on the garage wall. I threw hard to break it, but it came back every time I closed my eyes.

School started again in September, bringing long tedious days of math, English, science, and homework. My mind wandered out the open window to the ball diamond and Phil. He could hit the small chalked space almost every time now. I waited through each day for the final bell to ring, signaling my freedom to clutch the bat and swing time and time again at Phil's pitches. If I could learn to hit his, I could hit off any pitcher in the Little League.

Throughout that fall I hit the ball farther and farther. I learned to anticipate where the ball would cross the plate and know instinctively the moment to swing. Each time the ball soared past Phil or stung his hand through his padded glove, he smiled knowingly. For my thirteenth birthday I picked out my own baseball bat.

At times I felt Grandpa's Goliath growing in me. I was mad at him for showing it to me because I couldn't put its image out of my mind or stop Grandpa's voice within me.

It's pushing everything else out of your life, Seth.

"No, Grandpa!"

It's growing. It's growing every day you pick up that bat.

"No, Grandpa!"

Your grades are dropping, and you don't care.

"I'll bring them up."

It will engulf you. Fight it!

"All my new friends admire me because I'm good."

Your old ones are embarrassed when you come around.

"They don't play baseball."

You make them feel unworthy.

"Stop! I want to be the best!"

You've placed it above Him.

"No, Grandpa. I love Him. He's helping me."

Grandpa and Grandma came that Christmas to spend the rest of the winter and early spring with our family. I felt uncomfortable around Grandpa. I was sure he could see the black Goliath reflected in my eyes. I couldn't bear to see his apprehension every time I came in from practicing and laid my glove reverently on the shelf. Sooner or later I knew he was going to talk to me, knew he had more to say, something he had wanted to say last summer.

Spring tryouts were coming up. Phil and I wanted to make the Rams, a winning team that took only the best. Tryouts were held on a Saturday morning. Phil and I rode down to the diamond early enough to be the first ones there and practice one last time. We had been putting in at least three hours a day for the last two months, and all day Saturday. Phil's accuracy and speed were phenomenal, and I could hit everything he pitched to me and place it anywhere on the field. My only worry was fielding a spinning ground ball on a bad hop.

As the various managers began to arrive with the chalking equipment, I walked around the school to be alone. I wanted help before tryouts started. If I made the Rams, I could forego my trip to the ranch and play ball all summer. I circled the school and knelt in the bushes. When I stood up, I knew the help would be there.

Phil was the first to try out. He fired the ball past three hitters before one finally hit a dribbling grounder to the shortstop. I could see all the managers writing down his name and calculating what deals they would need to get him. Phil knew he had made the Rams as soon as he finished and sat down next to me.

"When you hit, I'll watch the managers. You can always tell who they want by the way they write while they're watching you."

We watched the other boys field and bat for another hour before I heard my name ring from the loudspeakers.

"Kill the ball, Seth. There isn't a kid out there who can pitch to you."

I caught every grounder they hit to me without a miss, then walked the few feet to homeplate and picked up the bat. The pitcher was an older boy who had played for the Rams the past two years. I knew if I could really get a piece of one he threw, my position on the team would be sure. I stepped into the batter's box and waited for that first throw. I wasn't going to let him get one past me. He stared down at me with that faint smile that said, "I hear you're good, kid, so here's the best I've got." I could taste the fear and excitement. Just before he threw the first pitch I could hear myself say, "Just this once, let me hit the ball over the fence."

The ball came; I clenched the bat high over my head. I could hear Phil's voice calling, "That's the one, Seth. Kill it!" I kept my position, waiting for the moment to bring the bat down, then put everything into that swing. The ball hit the bat squarely in the middle, and I watched it sail over the pitcher's head. I didn't run—I just stood there watching the ball climb higher and higher, over the second baseman's head, then the center fielder's, until finally it bounced ten feet beyond the fence.

"Run the bases, you clown!"

I obeyed, watching the managers writing furiously. I rounded the bases and smiled at the bewildered pitcher just before I crossed home plate and hugged Phil.

"What a hit! You clobbered it! You should have seen the managers' faces when that ball bounced into the street."

I grinned at him and ran to the bench to pick up my glove. We sat down, planning our season with the Rams, waiting for the end of try-outs.

The manager of the Rams stepped up to read the names, hesitating just long enough to let the suspense swell to unbearable heights.

"The following players have been selected to be this year's Rams. Seth Michaels . . ."

I didn't hear another name. Phil was assigned to another team. The manager told me that he had chosen me over Phil. He couldn't have us both. I picked up the Rams hat he handed me after practice, adjusted it to my head, and walked home higher and stronger than anything else in the world.

When I came home, I knew Grandpa wanted to talk to me. He waited until we were alone in the house. I was oiling my glove in the bedroom.

"Seth," he called. He was sitting on the couch with his thumb in the Book of Mormon. "I'd like to talk to you."

I kept on oiling my glove without looking at him until his silence drew my attention.

"You made your team?"

"Yes, sir. We just finished tryouts."

"You wanted to be the best last summer, Seth. Are you the best?"

"I think so, Grandpa. I hit the ball farther than anyone else."

He picked up my ball with his free hand and turned it in his palm. "My cousin was the best, too."

"Who was your cousin?"

He settled back into the chair, dropping the ball back into the glove. He stared at the ceiling as if the story was unfolding before him.

"He didn't play baseball because he lived in Denmark, but he could really play the violin. He practiced for hours because he wanted to be the lead violinist in Copenhagen and play at Tivoli Gardens. That was a great honor, so he didn't do anything else for years but play the violin. He became the best violinist in Copenhagen, and he was asked to play lead violin at Tivoli. He stayed the best for many years, but his bones got a disease in them, and he couldn't play as easily as before. Finally they wouldn't let him play at Tivoli anymore and someone else took his place. He had no family and no other interests. He walked around Copenhagen for days. Finally he climbed to the top of a five-story building.

"We have very steep roofs in Denmark to let the snow slide off. My cousin cleaned his violin, put it in the case, and then, holding it, slid headfirst down into the street. They buried him with the broken violin."

Grandpa rubbed his hands through his hair and stretched them behind his neck.

"Not a very happy story, is it, Seth? Your cousin Lauritz put all he was into his violin, and when it was gone, he had nothing left to stand on. You can't make one thing, or one talent, or one person a crutch, because if you do, heaven help you when that crutch is taken away."

I was silent. He could see the defiance in my eyes.

"Don't be mad at me, Seth. Don't hide."

"Why do you do this to me, Grandpa? Everytime I play I see your Goliath. You're ruining it for me. It's just a game."

"It's becoming more than a game for you. You're becoming like Lauritz."

"You're preaching to me, Grandpa, as if we were in church."

"Seth, I . . ."

"Now you're going to show me a scripture." I could see his thumb in the Book of Mormon. He opened it.

"There's a better way. Mormon showed it to us. Close your eyes and see it."

"Maybe I'm getting too old to do that anymore."

"Look at Mormon, Seth. When he was eleven, Mormon received charge of the gold plates. When he was fifteen, he had seen Christ, was almost an apostle, and tried to teach his fallen people. When he was sixteen, his character had become so refined that his people appointed him their leader."

I didn't want to hear any more, but still he continued.

"Be like Mormon and David. Beat Goliath."

"I've spent months practicing. Today I was the best at tryouts. Do you expect me to walk away from it because of a few scriptures and the story of a man who killed himself because he couldn't play the violin anymore?"

His head sagged on his chest.

"I'm sorry, Grandpa. I shouldn't talk to you that way."

"You're not fighting me, Seth. You're fighting yourself." He looked me full in the face and nothing I could do could hold it all together. "Seth, anyone can hit a ball with a stick. I expect you to build your ambitions on something that can never be taken away."

I didn't say another word to him, just rose and walked out the door and threw the baseball against the side of the garage. I threw the ball harder and harder, fighting to keep the giant out of my mind.

Two months passed, and Grandpa went back to Utah. Until he left I avoided him. It wasn't hard with all the practicing I was doing both before and after school. By the time he went home, I was hitting better and farther, and my pride was growing. Then the manager began to worry about my playing as part of a team.

Phil's team practiced early, and one day, on a spur-of-the-moment decision, Phil walked an extra two blocks to see the Rams practice. He arrived just as I picked up the bat.

I saw him climb the fence and smiled at him as he sat behind the backstop. He still inspired confidence in me even though I no longer needed his presence. I hit the first few pitches with an ease and self-assurance that sparked a mumbled discontent from the other players. I was used to it, even *liked* to hear it because it proved what I wanted to believe.

My manager called out, "Let me throw a few to him. Seth, you need a challenge. Step back into the batter's box."

Phil whispered through the wire of the backstop. "Don't let him get one past you, Seth. You can hit his pitches, too."

I turned and faced my manager, raising my bat to its accustomed position, waiting tensely for the first pitch. It came so fast I wasn't sure where it was going to cross the plate. I swung at a blur that sped across the center of the plate. I realized too late that it dipped below the bat just as I anticipated the knock of its impact. I heard the sound of the ball stinging its way into the catcher's mitt. "Strike one," he whispered to me.

The manager threw it twice more and struck me out, the first time in more than two months of practice. I dropped my bat and reached for my glove.

"No, Seth, stay in there until you hit one."

My confidence was shaken, but I picked up the bat determined to hit the next ball that crossed the plate. He read my eyes and threw one wild. I swung anyway.

"Strike four," the catcher whispered again.

Everyone tensed as they saw the contest taking shape. Phil stood behind the backstop telling me where I had gone wrong.

"Strike five."

"Strike six."

I dropped the bat again and walked behind the backstop.

"No, Seth, come on back. You haven't hit one yet. Let me pitch a few more."

"I can't hit it, Phil. He'll strike me out again."

"You're letting him get to you. Stay calm. I know you can hit his pitches. They're coming faster, that's all. Swing a little sooner."

"I can't hit them!"

"Come on back, Seth. You've got to hit one."

I gripped the bat in moist hands and faced the manager again. The other players glanced around the bases.

"Please!" I silently pleaded. "Don't let him strike me out again. Please, just this once let me hit one."

The ball spun through the air into the safety of the catcher's glove.

"Strike seven."

"Strike eight."

I struck out again and lowered the bat.

"Put it back on your shoulder and let me pitch you a few more. You still haven't hit one."

I returned the bat to my shoulder. It seemed to weigh a ton. Phil was silent now and sitting with his chin in his cupped hands. The ball sailed over the plate twice more before I realized I was all alone in a box that had become my sacred place. The manager threw another strike that brought the tally to twelve.

I battled for one hit time and time again, swinging wildly through a blur of tears. I ached for the tortured hissing of the ball and the sound of Phil pacing back and forth behind the backstop to end. Still strike after strike raced by me, and the image's black surface began to crack. I saw it and hated it.

The outfielders sat idly on the ground throwing rocks. Finally the manager threw one so slowly that I dribbled a grounder to first base and dropped the bat. I walked to where my glove lay on the ground by Phil's feet, not daring to look at him, not speaking to him, because I knew it was over, broken eternally beyond repair.

"Good-bye, Seth." His voice was distant, with a touch of empathy in it.

I picked up my glove without looking at him and walked past the second baseman and then the center fielder who tried over and over again to call me back. I walked past them all to the gate, where I stopped.

I felt an urge to return. I turned and faced the field, the players frozen in position. A force stung my eyes and lifted my head in fierce determination.

"I don't need it." I turned to the gate once again.

You cannot leave this way.

"I can! It's not important now."

It's more important now than ever.

"Let me go away with something. If I return, it wouldn't be the same. Phil would know."

Then you have learned nothing.

I tried to return, to make my feet obey, but they led me out the gate and home. I told my mother I had decided to give up the team and go to the ranch instead.

I never looked back on the ball diamond, but even so, Goliath was gathering, calling his broken pieces from the farthest corners of the field to stand black and shining again.

9

Diane and Jaimie

I was relieved to be at the ranch. I could ride there, withdraw into a world of sage and cattle. Baseball, strikeouts, Phil, and the nightmares faded into unreality with the oiled harnesses, the sound of the river, and the uneven light of the kerosene lanterns.

The first of the summer was glorious, even more so because of the barrenness of my last visit. All the joy of working side by side with my uncle, his gnarled hands, the worn leather, and the hot smell of sweat as we drove the teams returned with a deep serenity. I grew to love him even more that summer.

My third Sunday there Diane and Jaimie came. They were both from Oregon. I didn't know what relation they were to Aunt Pearl or Uncle Morgan. Visitors came and went all the time, many of them friends of friends. Jaimie and Diane were cousins to each other and came with their grandfather, who wanted to hunt chukars. They were both thirteen.

Diane was small and had midnight hair which ovaled her face, fine features, deep chocolate eyes, and a perfect set of teeth that made me wonder if she'd had braces. Her smile hinted at laughter that never came, and she painted her nails a soft pink. She took a bath in the house every day, which was a wonder to me as everyone else swam in the river most nights, and Aunt Pearl always sent a bar of soap with us. Diane's voice was calm and easy when she talked, which wasn't very often as she was shyer than I was. When anyone talked to her, she dropped her eyes and peeked up through her eyelashes when she thought you weren't looking. She was the prettiest girl I'd ever seen, and talking to her made me drop my eyes, too, and look for things to say written on my shoes. They were always covered with dust, however, so the words never came out right.

Jaimie was a little taller than Diane, which made her taller than I was by two inches. Her hair was longer than Diane's, rich and dark, rust-colored like autumn, except in the full sunlight. When she shook her head it spilled over her shoulders, lighter than air, to uncover two tiny pearl earrings white against the brown of her ears. She was a flurry of motion even when she lay down. She always sat with her right leg dropped over her left knee, bouncing the air with her foot in perfect rhythm. Her eyes were gem green ringed in white, and they could almost talk. I was certain they could read my thoughts, but I was never sure if she cared or knew what they were reading. She spoke to everyone, including the animals, in a voice that was clear and warm and that reached as high as the rimrock. I didn't search my shoes when I spoke to her. She swam in the river with us except on Saturday night, when she spent an eternity in the bathroom rolling her hair into a wonderment of curls for Sunday morning. I always waited for her to come out, trying to hide my anticipation from the watchful eyes of my cousins, but usually I fell asleep at the kitchen table and missed her exit.

The two of them spent most of their time together, and I was weak-kneed in love with them both from the first, feeling a silent energy inside that made me want to rip up trees and howl to the moon. I felt so full of power I could have built empires.

We were haying across the river during their visit. I was on the stack as usual and had fallen behind for thinking about them. By the time we stopped for lunch Monday afternoon, Uncle Morgan was on to me.

"What are you two girls going to do this afternoon while your grandpa's hunting?" he asked.

"We thought we'd cross the river and watch you hay."

"You can see a lot better from the top of the stack. Seth's got it half done. You wouldn't mind having two pretty girls up on the stack with you, would you, Seth?"

"It's not really that fun, and the hay makes you itch."

"Oh, I think that sounds great!" Jaimie answered.

"Watch out for his pitchfork, though. When Seth starts moving hay, nobody's safe."

So it began. They sat in the hay through three more stacks in the following days, Jaimie laughing and throwing timothy spears, always in my way, and Diane sitting on the edge of the stack, humming and watching the hawks circle. I never once fell behind, and every stack was squared up perfectly.

Early one morning when Uncle Morgan was alone, I followed him down to do the chores. He was balancing on the one-legged stool, his hat mashed against the cow's side while his hands brought forth the milk smoothly.

"Talk, I'm listening," he said.

"It's hard."

He stopped milking and twisted his head to look up at me, his hat still smashed against the cow.

"Is it time for that talk already?" he asked.

"What talk?"

"There's a talk I guess you're about old enough to be hearing."

"About girls?"

"That's the one."

"I've already had that one."

"Oh? Who gave it to you?"

"Grandpa."

"And what did he tell you?"

"He started with Adam and Eve and told me about my name. I even remember the scripture. 'And Adam knew his wife again; and she bare a son, and called his name Seth.' There's another one that says 'in his own likeness, after his image.' They're all in Genesis."

"That sounds like a good way to do it. Since you've already had that talk, what can I do for you?"

He bent back over the milk pail, and the milk pinged the sides once again.

"You know Jaimie and Diane?"

"Yes, it seems like I've heard those names."

"I like them both. I don't mean like, I mean *really* like."

"Oh, that kind of like."

"Is it okay?"

"To like someone?"

"No, to like two at the same time."

"You like them both that much?"

"Jaimie's fun to be around, and I can talk to her. I want to climb the mountains with her, but Diane is prettier, and I go all soft inside when she looks at me."

"It's that bad?"

"Is it bad?"

"Not at your age."

"Can you like both, or do you have to decide?"

"I'll think on it."

"You don't know now?"

"This is a deep problem. I don't think anybody's ever had a problem quite like this. It takes thought, but I'll get back with you."

A day later he called me to him after lunch. "Go down to the barn, Seth, and bring me an empty grain sack."

"What do you need it for?"

"You need it."

"I need it?"

"Just run and get it. A good one with no holes."

I came back five minutes later with the best sack I could find.

"Now take this pair of gloves—they're good heavy ones. Follow the rake as it puts the hay into windrows. There will be lots of mice. They're easy to catch. Catch me a sackful while I go find Molly."

"Is this like snipe hunting?"

"You'll see—just go get the mice."

I crossed the river and headed for the rake. Jaimie and Diane saw me and came over.

"What's the sack for?"

"Mice."

"How horrible, Jaimie. Let's go back."

"You go on, I want to watch."

Diane ran back across the river, and I walked on with Jaimie.

"What do you want mice for?"

"They're for Uncle Morgan."

"What's he going to do with them?"

"I don't know. He just told me to catch a bunch with these gloves."

We reached the rake. As the teeth pulled the hay up, the mice darted through the cut stalks. Uncle Morgan was right—there were hundreds of them. I caught over fifty in less than a half hour with Jaimie screaming every minute, "There's another one!" Every few minutes I had to shake them down to the bottom of the sack. The sack could have crawled away on its own power had I put it on the ground.

"I guess I have enough. Let's go back."

"Can I watch?"

"You'll have to ask Uncle Morgan."

He was sitting on the front porch with Molly curled up in his lap. She was the oldest cat on the ranch and the best mouser we had.

"Did you get enough?"

"More than fifty."

"That's plenty. Let's go down to the corral."

"Can Jaimie watch?"

"Jaimie, this is man's work. Seth and I have to have a man's talk. I think this time you should stay here."

She frowned, but her eyes danced with light. "Oh," she said. That one expression held the universe. Her eyes stared so knowingly that I opened the sack and shook the mice down again. When I peeked up, she was still looking at me.

"Let's go, Seth."

He slung Molly over his arm. She hung there placidly as though she were held together with fur and fat, not muscle and bone.

"Keep the mice down so Molly won't smell them until we get to the barn. I don't want her to have a fit when I'm holding her."

We climbed the corral, and he led me to the center, where he put Molly down.

"Let her smell the sack."

I lowered it to her nose. She went stiff as a sawhorse, then began batting the bottom of the sack with both paws.

"Dump them out and step back."

He moved about ten yards away while I tipped the sack upside down. The ground became a motion of fur with one mountain of grayness a foot high in the center. Molly exploded into the middle of it, burying her face up to the ears in squealing frenzy. She came up a split second later with a mouse in her teeth. The mountain started melting, with mice running everywhere. Molly began swatting and batting every mouse that ran by. She dropped the mouse in her teeth and decided on another one, which she dropped a second later as another scurried from between her paws. She tried to hold one with each paw, but they wiggled out and raced away. Little explosions of dust billowed with every swipe and wreathed her in chalky brown. Uncle Morgan and I howled with laughter as she tried to gather mice with her front paws as a casino gambler gathers chips. When that didn't work, she banged her paws down a dozen times in less than a dozen seconds, each time rolling a mouse in the dust. Mice were all over the corral, slipping into holes and climbing fence posts. Within a minute they were all gone, and Molly was alone in the middle of the corral. A solitary mouse hung from beneath her whiskers, and her normal yellow color was a confusion of browns. It took another three minutes for either of us to stop laughing. Finally, Uncle Morgan sat down in the dirt and patted the ground next to him.

"Sit down, Seth."

I squatted next to him, wiping the tears from my eyes.

"What did you learn?"

"About what?"

"About your problem."

"I don't know. I thought it was funny. What's it got to do with Diane and Jaimie?"

"Look at Molly." He was still smiling, and mischief pulled at the corners of his eyes. "How many mice did she catch?"

"Just one—the rest got away."

"But she swatted at a bunch of them, didn't she? She even dropped some she caught first to go for another one. That's the way love is, Seth. We're like Molly there. We swat a few here and a few there and try to catch them, but in the end we settle on one and let the others go. You've just begun to swat. You're a few years away from doing any catching, but you can swat all you want."

"Does that mean it's all right to like them both?"

"It means until you're sixteen you won't need to worry about it, and by then these two mice will be long gone."

"Is that the way it was with you and Aunt Pearl?"

"Sometimes I think I was the mouse, and she did all the swatting."

"That's what Grandpa said about Grandma."

"Well, he's a smart man, your grandpa, but right now we'd better be going. You've got a little green-eyed girl up there wanting to know what you did with fifty mice."

"Uncle Morgan?"

"Yes."

"I still think I need to make a choice."

"Well, I can see you won't let it rest, so I'll think on it some more."

A few days later, Uncle Morgan was showing Jaimie and Diane's grandfather his arrowheads. We all gathered around to see the black and red flints. Both Diane and Jaimie expressed an interest in them, and by the time the conversation was over I was appointed to take the two of them and their grandfather to a cave down in the canyon where the Indians used to live.

Diane talked to me all the way down the trail. I was glad we were riding, because her voice still turned my legs to soft butter. We found lots of chips, clam shells from ancient feasts, and a few points, but Jaimie found a white, narrowly flaked awl that fanned out like a scallop on top and tapered down to a fine point three inches below. Uncle Morgan said he could still hear the Indian screaming who had lost it. It was beautiful, and I never coveted anything so badly in my life.

We were covered with fine dust from the cave floor when we got back to the ranch. Diane went inside to take a bath, but Jaimie came down to the river with me to swim. We lay down in the middle of the river and let the current wash the dirt from our clothes. The water was cool, and I could hear the mower cutting and smell the hay as it came with the breeze.

"Do you like it out here, Seth?"

"More than anything. I wish I could live here all year."

"Your folks would miss you."

"My mother would."

"Just your mother?"

"My parents are divorced."

"Do you visit your father?"

"I used to see him when I was little. He'd take us to Lagoon, but since I've been coming out here I don't see him anymore."

"Do you miss him?"

"How can you miss what you've never had?"

"I'd miss my dad."

"What's he like?"

"Fun to be with, like your Uncle Morgan, always teasing."

"Do you remember what he was like when you were little? I mean really little, like one or two?"

"I remember he took me and my brother for a walk one day in some woods behind our house. I picked some flowers off a bush that had a hornet's nest in it. They began to sting me. Dad put me under one arm and my brother under the other and ran down the road with us. The hornets swarmed after us, but he outran them. When we got home, he put Band-Aids on all my stings and held me in his arms until the hurting stopped and I went to sleep."

"You remember all that?"

"Sure."

"Do you remember other things?"

"Lots of them."

"Tell me."

96

"Oh, carving pumpkins on Halloween, and trick or treating, putting on shows for him in the basement, playing Rook with Dad as my partner and never knowing when to play the rook."

"Did he laugh?"

"All the time. Do you wish you had a dad, Seth?"

She rolled over in the water and looked at me, and her eyes went soft. Mine did too, so I ducked under the water and held my breath. When I came up she was still looking.

"I have Uncle Morgan and Grandpa and someone else."

"Who?"

"I never talk about it."

"Oh."

She ducked under the water this time and came up flipping water with her hair.

"Will you take me fishing tomorrow?"

"I guess if you want to."

"I can bait my own hook."

"What about Diane?"

"She doesn't like to fish."

"We can't go for very long. I have to stack tomorrow."

"That's okay."

I ducked under the water again and felt its coolness fit me like another skin. When I came up, Jaimie was walking back to the house. Diane was standing by the willows. The blood drained from my hands and feet, but I found the strength to walk with her back to the house.

"Uncle Morgan, did you think on it long enough?"

"Is it that desperate?"

"I think so."

"You think you've swatted enough mice?"

"For now."

"I'm going to have to let you in on my secret, then. It was given to me by my father and I imagine his father before that. You won't tell anyone, will you?"

"I'll keep it a secret."

"If it got around to too many people, it wouldn't work anymore."

"I promise."

"You'll wait until you're sixteen? I wouldn't want your mother mad at me."

"They're both going home in two days. I'll probably never see them again."

"Then why is it so important?"

"For the memory."

"I see. Come with me, then."

We walked over to the barn, and he picked up the old work gloves and the grain sack.

"You're sure you want to go through with this?"

"I'm sure."

"Then I'm going to need some more mice."

"Do you want me to find Molly?"

"No, we don't need her this time. Just two mice. You go catch two and meet me at the dam above the house."

He was waiting for me when I crossed over the log that formed the main support of the dam. "Did you get two?"

"They're in the sack."

"Let me see if they're good enough."

He peered into the sack for a good minute.

"They'll do fine."

"What are you going to do with them?"

"Race them. You've got the gloves on. Pick one up in each hand by the back of the neck."

I reached into the sack while he held it open for me, and I grabbed a mouse in each hand.

"Look at them good, Seth, and name them. One for Diane and one for Jaimie."

"This one's . . ."

"Think hard."

I looked at the two mice hanging limp from my fingers. "This one's Diane, she's smallest. This one's Jaimie, she's a little bigger."

"Now put them in the water above the dam. The first one to the other side is the one you remember. Okay?"

"Okay."

"Seth."

"Yes?"

"The right one always wins."

I placed them in the water. They took off for the other side, churning the water into miniature bubbles and leaving tiny wakes across the still water. They streamed to the other bank side by side, moving slowly downstream as they went.

"Nobody's winning."

"Take it easy. Pretty good little swimmers, aren't they?"

"They're almost there."

"Who's ahead?

"I can't tell."

"Looks like the big one is pulling ahead. Which one was that?"

"Jaimie," I whispered. "Come on, Jaimie, you can do it!"

She crawled onto the bank a full two lengths ahead of Diane and darted into the weeds.

"She won, Uncle Morgan, she won!"

"I thought you were having trouble deciding?"

"I thought I was too."

"Is that why you made the bigger mouse Jaimie?"

"Was I cheating?"

"It doesn't matter. The mice are never wrong."

"Never?"

"Never, but don't tell anyone. Besides, I knew Jaimie would win all along."

"How?"

"She was the one you wanted to climb mountains with."

"Uncle Morgan?"

"Yes."

I couldn't say it. I picked up a rock and skipped it across the still water of the dam. He skipped one too, then said, "Let's go home."

10

A Father's Love

We left early the next morning before the sun rose to get the mares ready to take to the Gillette ranch. Not everyone could fit in the cab, so three of us climbed up the wooden slats of the cattle truck and clung to the top of the cab. Here we could ride for hours while the truck bumped along the gravel roads. My cousin Dan rode in the front to get the gates.

We stopped while we were driving to allow Dan to fire a random round at groundhogs. He drew the bolt back and sighted down the barrel, but before he could fire, the squirrel had ducked back into his hole. Dan snapped the safety into place, tested the trigger, and climbed back into the truck. He leaned the .22 against the cab door so it would be ready the next time.

The slow, lumbering shaking of the truck and the idle drone of the engine put Dan to sleep. The .22 banged against the cab door, loosening the catch on the safety and knocking the gun against his side. We came to a gate, and Uncle Morgan stopped the truck so Dan could climb out and open it. As he opened the door the rifle slid out on the ground, jamming the firing pin against the running board. I heard a shot and looked down from my perch just in time to see Dan slump to the ground.

For a second or two we were all too shocked to move. Uncle Morgan tore out of the truck, circled the cab, and rushed to Dan's side. He was conscious but in a great deal of pain. As Uncle Morgan rolled him over and cradled him in his arms I saw blood trickle slowly down his side.

It was quiet—so quiet I could hear the rushing of a stream through the trees in the distance. Dan didn't say anything. He looked into his father's face, a question fleeting across his eyes. The silence became unreal and unbearably long. Uncle Morgan shifted Dan's body a bit to make him more comfortable, and in doing so he pulled his arm from behind his back. It was covered with blood. The bullet had gone through Dan's body. Nobody had to tell me that Dan was hurt badly.

Then came a sound I will never forget. From somewhere deep within my uncle's chest an animal-like sob of fear and hurt pushed through. It cut the heavy air, engulfing the silence, knocking the breath out of me more forcefully than any blow. I watched the rhythmic shaking of his body as the sobs tore through him.

Then Dan was crying, trying hard to hold it in, trying to carry the burden, but crying with the fear of death and the anguished look of his father. For that one moment in time, frozen in my memory, father and son were one. Then I was crying, but not for Dan. I was fighting the revelation that was staring at me from those dust-filled ruts, a revelation I didn't want to accept. I remembered a tangled mat of sagebrush and the running figure of my uncle.

"Somebody get me some water," Uncle Morgan pleaded.

I had to look into his eyes. I would know if I could look into his eyes, but from where I was standing they were hidden by the sweat-soaked brim of his hat. I slid from the cab without taking my eyes off the wedded figures in the road and crouched down beside my uncle.

"Seth! I need some water!"

I looked at his hand as it lay over the open wound. He was trying to hold in the life that was pulsing its way out through his fingers.

"Seth! Please hurry!"

I had to look.

"Seth!"

I got up without looking, ran to the stream, and filled a can with water. I tried to walk up the hill without spilling any, but my hands were shaking and the water was splashing down my shirt. I had seen the naked love of a father for a son, and I knew that I'd never see that same depth of love in my uncle's eyes for me. The physical emptiness I had felt from time to time returned.

"Where's the water?"

I brought the water to him, then circled the truck and slumped down by a back tire.

He's his son! I can't expect it to be the same for me.

I looked up to see a small cloud of dust in the horizon. A car was coming our way. My cousins flagged it down and asked the driver for help. They placed Dan in the back seat, and Uncle Morgan climbed in with him. The car became a cloud of dust again, and we were alone on the dirt road.

Somewhere between the gate where Dan had been shot and the ranch the numbness inside of me turned rock hard.

We got to the ranch. I slid off the cab and started up the hill. Everyone came out of the house asking a hundred questions and demanding a hundred different answers. I didn't wait for them. Jaimie ran after me and caught me a few yards up the trail.

"Where are you going?" Her hard breathing troubled her voice.

I didn't stop for her, didn't even speak to her. I just kept climbing. Halfway up the hill I sat by a rock and stared across the valley. Jaimie was still standing in the yard looking up at me. There were no tears, no pain now; only a war waged within myself.

I hated my father for leaving. I wouldn't have needed Uncle Morgan if he had stayed with us. All the memories my mother had planted were lies. Dad never cared for us. All we were to him was a convenient envelope with scribbled checks. I wanted more. I wanted to look into a human face, into a father's eyes, and see a father's love. Life had cheated me out of that—now it was taking my Uncle Morgan. I'd never had him in the first place, but I had a memory, misinterpreted but better than nothing.

Other memories came like little breakers, steady, soaking through the sands of my emotions. The two sunbleached piles of bones passed through my mind, and I recalled my uncle's voice. "It does no good to think of the bad, Seth, the pain and the hurt. We learn from them and go on. Now I ride by and think of the fifteen years."

Hours later I came down from the dark mountainside remembering my few years. Jaimie and Diane were gone with their grandfather to see Dan in the hospital; then they were going back to Oregon. When I crawled into bed that night the white awl, carefully wrapped in cotton, was on my pillow.

11

Walk without Fear

My best friend during the next few years was a boy named Mark. He was as small as I was, had thick, dirty blond hair and dark brown eyes. He was hard to get to know because he didn't talk much until he trusted you. He had one thing I envied—a deep bass voice. My own voice sounded as though I were speaking through a straw. It was strange to hear such a resonant voice coming from such a little body. When I got to know him better, he mimicked newscasters and TV stars, announcing common events as if they were world-shaking news. He was a picky eater and the only person I knew who ate peanut butter sandwiches on Thanksgiving because he didn't like turkey or dressing. He seemed put together with bits of other people. He always said, "God made me out of everything He had left over after creating everyone else." He was the only person with whom I shared most of my experiences.

Mark and I shared the common legacy of being reared solely by our mothers. His mother was trying to get married again. He told me how awkward it was for him to meet the different men his mother went out with. He thought it strange that my own mother had decided not to re-marry.

"Don't you want another father?" he asked me one day. That's when I first told him about my rat and how I no longer wanted my father. We had some long talks about that, and he asked me a lot of questions, but after a while the talks became less frequent.

Mark moved into our ward the middle of my eighth-grade year. I grew closer to him after my friendship with Phil ended. We set a goal of becoming Eagle Scouts, and we worked on merit badges together, sharing long hours in the fields and mountains obtaining the same ranks and standing side by side at each court of honor.

I didn't know what it meant to be hated then, but he did. One day his enemies caught up with him on my front lawn. The two of them were both bigger than we were, and they were schooled in the art of street fighting. Mark didn't have a chance.

"You owe us," one of them shouted.

"I haven't got my paper route anymore."

He broke from them and ran, getting only as far as my front porch, when they grabbed him and pulled him onto the front lawn. They hit him hard with their fists.

"Come on, Mark, fight!" they shouted at him.

After the first few blows he crumpled to the ground, shielding his face and stomach from the hailstorm of blows. I could hear him crying. I wanted to help him but I couldn't. I stood there watching, ashamed and guilty, doing nothing but feeling the fear rising in my throat like sandpaper.

I didn't know how to fight. I'd never learned. "Coward!" I derided myself.

My older sister came out of the house.

"Help him, Jan! You're a girl. They won't do anything to you."

She turned the sprinklers on and then beat them with a hose before they stopped. They laughed and ran down the street. I felt a brassy taste in my mouth and tried to stop the shaking inside me. I couldn't move off the porch until they rounded the corner and the shaking stopped.

Mark was sitting on the lawn with his face in his hands. Jan tried to get him to stop crying and come to the house, but he wanted to go home. Blood trickled through his fingers, and welts on his arms and back pushed through the wet transparency of his T-shirt.

"Go call his mother, Jan."

I sat down next to him on the wet grass.

"I should have helped you, Mark. I didn't know what to do. They threw me back on the porch."

"It's all right, Seth. They would have beat you up too."

"I should have helped even if they beat me up."

"You couldn't have done anything."

"It wasn't fair, two against one. Who were those guys anyway?"

"Hoods."

He took his hands from his face and looked down the street. A large lump had formed on the side of his head, and his lip was cracked in two places.

"I'm going to get even."

"You're too small, Mark, and there are two of them."

"It doesn't matter if you know how to fight."

Jan cleaned him up before his mother came and drove him home. I turned to my sister.

"Jan."

"What?"

"Thanks. I should have—"

"Don't even say it. You couldn't have done anything. You're smaller than he is. Don't worry about it."

She went back into the house.

"I wanted to help him," I told myself.

There was only silence.

"I was afraid. So I did nothing."

I gathered the hose together and laid the coils on the porch.

Still our friendship grew, although I found it harder and harder to work with him on our last merit badges. He was spending most of his time with another boy from school who was teaching him how to fight.

"I'm getting good, Seth," he said to me one day while we were hiking.

"Good at what?"

"Fighting. Nobody is going to beat me up again."

"Why do you want to learn how to fight?"

"You saw what they did to me."

"Yes, but . . . "

"Well, it's not ever going to happen again."

"But there were two of them, and they've got other friends. There's a whole gang of them."

"I've got friends too . . ." He paused seeing the effect of his words. "I mean—"

"No, I deserved it. I should have helped you."

"That's just it. You don't know how to fight. They would have beat you up too, just like they did me."

"Do you like that new kid you've been hanging around with lately?"

"He knows how to fight. If my dad had stuck around, he could have shown me. I've got to learn from someone. My mother thinks it's okay. You'd better learn, too."

I tried to picture myself fighting. "As long as I don't get in their way I'll be all right."

"I used to think that way too."

I avoided the hoods for a while until I took a shop class that made it impossible for me to stay out of their way. Most of them were in it. I didn't know what they called themselves, but their emblems were a blue tanker jacket, which made their shoulders and arms look twice as big as they really were, and a dirty white T-shirt. Twelve of them were in the class.

The shop teacher was almost retired and knew from the beginning he was going to have trouble with them. He wore dark-rimmed glasses that dipped over his nose and was the only teacher in the school whose hair was all white. Everyone called him the "Bald Eagle." Rather than fight the entire gang, he chose to close his eyes to their activities and spent most of the period in his office. We called it "The Nest." An unwritten code seemed to exist between him and them, an established compromise. I knew he was afraid of them too because whenever they looked at him he cleaned his glasses and ran his thumb and finger over the thin gray line of his mustache.

I tried to change my schedule, but the principal wouldn't hear of it. I couldn't tell him my fears, because they had done nothing, but I could sense their restlessness and knew they were only waiting for a chance. I was determined not to give them that chance.

One day the two boys who beat up Mark ditched a class and entered the shop. They recognized me and came over to where I was working. I was building a maze and cages for the science fair.

"You that chicken kid that sat on the front porch and let his sister fight his battles?"

I could feel the blood pounding through my body. I didn't say a word, just kept working on my project.

"Hey, I'm talking to you!"

He grabbed my arm and pushed my project away. I could smell the tobacco on his breath. A few of his friends were gathering.

"This is the kid I was telling you about. He just stood there and let us beat up his friend."

"I haven't done anything to you."

"You'd better not or you know what you'll get, don't you? We'll make sure there's no sister to run crying to."

That was all it took to start it. Every day they were at me, trying to pick a fight. I tried my best to stay out of their way and do what they wanted. I wasn't careful enough.

"Hey, I need that saw," he yelled to me from across the shop.

"I'm almost done. I'll bring it in just a minute."

I had made a mistake. I would have taken it back, but it was too late—he was on his way over. The whole shop stopped.

"You talking back to me? I said I needed the saw."

He stood a whole foot taller than I. I gave him the saw. He turned to go, then whirled around and kicked me in the stomach. All eyes turned to where I was doubled over. I looked for the teacher. He was in the office talking to another boy, and I knew it was a setup. The other boys turned slowly and continued working on their projects. I knew how it felt for Mark when I just stood on the front porch. The brassy sensation I had felt that day returned, and I began to shake inside. I stayed doubled over, pretending it still hurt even after the pain was gone. He finally left me and walked away. The shop returned to normal.

I waited for the bell to ring so I could go home. I let them all leave first, hoping I wouldn't have to walk across the parking lot with them, but they were waiting for me when I came out the door. The boy who kicked me filled his mouth with Coke. When I walked by, he spit it all over me and laughed.

"Oh, I'm sorry. Look, I got Coke all over you. I just had to sneeze as you were walking by. You're all wet and sticky."

One of his friends yelled, "Hey, I wouldn't let anybody do that to me. Come on, fight him!"

"You want to fight, kid? Come on, I'm ready for you."

I backed away, then turned and ran. He chased me, filled his mouth with Coke again, and sprayed my back as I turned around the shop building corner.

I hated them with every step I took. I hated them more because I was afraid of them and they knew it. Mark was right—you couldn't stay away from them. I needed to learn how to fight. If I could beat one of them, they would leave me alone, but how could I ever learn how to fight? They were all older and stronger, and I was small. I hadn't grown an inch in two years.

I got home from school before anyone else. I showered a long time, rubbing the soap across my back and shoulders with a vigor that left them sore and red. I had stepped out of the shower and changed into clean clothes before the trembling stopped. I picked up my stained shirt and took it to the incinerator. I could never wear it again. I lit a match and waited for the flames to get big. I threw the shirt in and watched it burn.

"I hate you, and I'm going to get even. I'll get you back!" I shouted it to the incinerator and savored the thought as though it had already been accomplished.

"I'm going to learn to fight even if I'm too small. Maybe He'll help me grow if I ask Him—no, I'll do it on my own."

I studied the swirling mass of black smoke coming from the shirt.

"I'll never learn. All I can do is burn shirts and run. It means nothing."

I heard a car drive up. Mother was home from school. I faced the burnt cinders.

What do I do tomorrow? I can't go back. It will be even worse. I hate them. What will I do when they come after me again? I know they will.

The voice came faintly. *Endure.*

I closed the incinerator door, trying to be strong, to have faith, to stop hating, to endure, but the fear was still inside. I saw Grandpa standing by the corner of the garage. I tried to walk by him as if nothing had happened.

"Hi, Grandpa. I heard a car—Mother must be home."

"Why did you burn your shirt, Seth?"

I stopped. "You saw me?"

"Yes, and I heard you showering."

"I got Coke all over it. It was ruined."

"I know." He said it with resignation and disappointment. I remembered Uncle Jens.

"I didn't drink it, Grandpa. I'm not trying to hide anything."

He knew I was telling the truth and relaxed. "How did you get Coke on you?"

"Do I have to tell you?"

"Not if you don't want to."

He looked hurt, shifted his suspenders, coughed.

"Somebody spit it on me. He wanted to fight, but I ran away. I'm a coward."

He didn't face me for a moment. "There's not always shame in running, Seth."

"There's shame in hating."

"Do you hate them?"

"I'm trying not to."

"How many were there?"

"How did you know there were more than one?"

"Things haven't changed that much in eighty years."

"There were about ten."

"Why do you suppose they are that way?"

"I don't know. They're born mean, I guess."

"If you could figure out why they're that way you might not hate them. You might pity them."

"I don't think I'll ever pity them."

"I don't believe that. An obsession with hatred, Seth, can fill your soul, become your god." He paused for a moment. "Did it make you feel any better to burn your shirt?"

"A little."

"I used to pound nails."

"When?"

"When I got mad and couldn't do anything."

"Did it help?"

"Not much. Maybe I'll burn a shirt next time if you recommend it."

"No, pounding nails sounds better. Is that why you became a carpenter?"

"Well, I wasn't mad that much."

"Grandpa, you're not going to tell Mother are you? It was a good shirt."

"Not if you don't want me to."

He put his arm around me, and we walked to the house. He said something in Danish clear and loud, not under his breath as he usually did. He pulled me next to him as we walked.

"What does that mean, Grandpa?"

"Those that are with us are more than those that are against us."

I recognized the story. I had heard him tell it more than once, and he referred to it in the book Mother typed for me. I wanted to believe him, but I was not Elisha. Nor did I have my grandfather's faith in the scriptures. I knew the fear was still inside me, that it would be even stronger tomorrow when I went back to school.

I found Mark the next day and told him. I had to talk with someone my age who had been through it.

"Are you going back?"

"I have to. What else can I do?"

"You can tell someone."

"That would just make them madder, and it would be worse."

"You can get a friend like mine."

"I don't think so, Mark."

"I told you it would happen sooner or later. They look for you if you're small. There's no way out of it."

"Maybe they'll leave me alone today."

"They won't. It'll be worse every day."

"I haven't got any other choice. I can't ditch every class."

"Then learn to fight, and one day you can give it back to them."

"I guess I'll just take my chances."

"Those hoods spit Coke all over you, and you're not going to do anything?"

I tried to explain it to him, but I couldn't get the words out right. I wasn't sure I understood it myself. I felt He didn't want me to fight. I told Mark about the incinerator and hating people.

"You're going back there and let them push you around?"

"I guess so."

"If that's the Church's idea of God—"

"I didn't say it was the Church's idea."

"Well, what does it mean then?"

"I don't know exactly."

"Even Christ kicked them out of the temple."

"That was different."

"How different?"

I felt there was something I should say to him, but I didn't know what.

"I'll be late for class, Mark. Wait for me after school."

They were waiting for me when I came into the shop. The teacher was in "The Nest." They gathered around.

"I see you took a bath. You want another shower today? I thought I cleaned you up pretty good."

"Why don't you leave me alone? I never did anything to you."

"You wasted some of my Coke yesterday. Hey! How much Coke you guys think I wasted cleaning this kid up yesterday?"

"At least a nickel's worth." It was his best friend.

"I figure you owe me a nickel like my buddy here says. That's fair, ain't it?"

They gathered closer around me, their blue tanker jackets puffed out around the white of their stained T-shirts.

Father, help. I can't go through it again, I prayed.

"Yeah, you owe me a nickel."

I took out a nickel and gave it to him. He turned it over and over in his fingers and slipped it into his pocket.

"You bring me one every day, and we'll leave you alone."

Mark was waiting for me in the parking lot after school, and we walked home together.

"What happened in shop?"

"They're going to leave me alone."

"Just like that? They didn't say anything?"

I couldn't tell him about the nickel because I knew what he would say and I didn't want to justify it. I wasn't sure I had made the right decision, but they didn't bother me the rest of the period. It was worth a nickel.

"They pushed me around a little, but it's going to be okay now."

"Are you sure?"

"Would I say so if I wasn't?"

The last thing I checked before I left for school each morning was the nickel in my pocket. It was the most important thing I had to remember. I thought about it more than books, homework, or lunch. Once I forgot it and ran back eight blocks to get it. I was late for school, without an excuse, but it didn't matter. I had to have that nickel. They left me alone for two weeks. Sometimes they even let me keep the nickel, but they asked to see it every day. I was beginning to feel more comfortable in class, and the fear didn't grip me as badly when I walked across the parking lot to the shop building.

12

"Those Who Are with Us"

I had only six weeks to go when the final incident occurred. I was working on my science fair project, a wooden maze that helped me compare the intelligence of a mouse, a rat, and a hamster. Every day I clocked them as they tried to learn the twists, doors, and turns it took to get to the food at the end. I won the school competition and was given the opportunity of going to the all-school event. The hoods heard about it and tried to spoil it.

As I was taking my project home they caught up with me three blocks from school. In the hazing that followed, they took the mouse out of its cage and played catch with him. Somebody missed, and he fell to the sidewalk. When I finally got him home he wasn't moving very much. If he died, the project was ruined.

I pleaded with my mother to let me keep him in the house for a few nights. I told her he was sick. I promised her he wouldn't get loose. "I'll lock him in the bathroom inside a box."

I convinced her, and she let me bring the mouse into the bathroom, to my grandmother's loud disapproval. I couldn't bring the cage in, so I made a nest for the mouse in a small wooden crate. He was still quiet.

I went to sleep praying the mouse would be better. When I lifted the box lid in the morning, I found a little hole in the corner, and the mouse was gone. I searched the bathroom with no luck.

I didn't know how I was going to tell my mother. She came into my room when I was on my knees looking under the bookcase and guessed what had happened. If it had been anything but a mouse, life would have been easier. Mother couldn't stand mice, and my grandmother had an instant fit.

"Seth! You're not going to school today. I'm going to take the day off and take your grandparents to the mountains. When I come back this evening, I want that mouse in its cage in the garage!"

She stormed out of the room with Grandma huffing behind her. Grandpa shrugged and followed them into the kitchen. Before she left she said, "When you look for that mouse, remember the last place you think he'd be is the first place you want to look."

I spent the whole day going from room to room without any success. I found an old slipper I'd lost three years before, a baseball, Mother's good ballpoint pen, and some old Christmas decorations, but no mouse.

For days everybody tiptoed around, but no one saw anything. Mother's anger soon turned to worry when she realized that without the mouse, there would be no all-school competition. We both feared the mouse had crawled into a corner and died.

Each day that I looked in vain for the mouse my hate increased. I still brought the nickels, but they could tell my attitude had changed and pushed harder to get me to fight.

"You hate me, don't you?" It was always the boy who spit the Coke. I wondered if they had assigned him to pick on me.

"Yes! You ruined my project!"

"Oh, I'm sorry. Did your little mouse die?"

I didn't want to tell him he got loose so I said nothing. He hooted in delight. "Maybe that hate will be enough to stop your chicken blood, and you won't run away every time class is over."

Every day I'd remember the incinerator and try not to hate.

One morning Mother called to me excitedly. I ran into the kitchen and found her looking into the cupboard.

"Look, Seth. The mouse must still be alive!"

I climbed on a chair and looked at where Mother was pointing. Several mouse droppings were by the butter, and one corner of it had been nibbled on.

"He's still alive. Maybe we can catch him in time for you to go to the science fair," she said.

We saw him quite frequently during the next few days. He'd dart across the living room and dive under the bookcase. Pandemonium always broke loose as everyone scrambled for higher ground except Grandpa and I. Sometimes we saw him during dinner when he dove under the refrigerator. We saw him often, but no one could catch him.

Four days before the science fair I was full of hate. They sensed it and kept at me constantly. Mark pushed me to let his friend teach me how to fight.

I could tell they were plotting something that week by the way they cast glances back and forth during the period. I could also tell it didn't involve me because they forgot to ask for the nickel.

They waited until the teacher was in his office before they took the gasoline out of their coat pockets and moved slowly to the buffers. I ignored them, grateful that they were occupied with something else. I never saw who actually lit the fire. When I looked the buffers were spinning and shooting flames four feet high. It looked like the Fourth of July. Everyone yelled at once.

"Fire!"

"Clear the building!"

"We're going to be burned alive!"

"Ring the alarm. I don't want to die. We've got to get out!"

One of them rang the fire alarm. The teacher bolted out of his office. He grabbed the fire extinguisher off the wall and tried to get the pin out. They had soldered it in. He turned the buffers off, burning his hand, and put the flames out with water from the bathroom. When the fires were out, he canceled the alarm.

He made us all sit on our benches and face him. The truce was broken.

"All right, boys, who set the buffers on fire?"

Nobody said a word, and the bell rang. They had timed it perfectly.

"I'm going to find out who lit it, and when I do I'll see that that person never sets foot in this school again."

They filed out, bursting into laughter when they reached the middle of the parking lot.

My grandparents left for Utah that morning, and my mother returned to her own room. About three in the morning, the mouse crawled up the bedspread onto the extra pillow next to her. She woke and felt something move next to her head. When she tried to reach for the light the mouse ran across her hand and chest. Squelching her rising panic, she clicked the light on. The mouse cowered in a fold of the bedspread. She called for me to come, but my bedroom was at the other end of the house, and I was a heavy sleeper.

The mouse moved. Mother scooped it up, holding it loosely, trying not to squeeze it. "Seth! I've got the mouse, come quickly!"

The mouse turned inside her hands. "He's going to bite me!"

She shook her hands rapidly, bouncing the mouse from side to side so it couldn't bite her. "Seth! Wake up!"

She struggled to get out from under the covers. When she was finally free, she rushed down the hall and into my room.

"Seth! The mouse! Wake up!" She flicked my light with her elbow and kicked the bed with her foot. I finally woke up, but the light was too strong for my eyes. I couldn't see a thing. "For heaven's sake, hurry! I've got the mouse."

"Huh?"

Mother was still shaking her hands when my eyes finally focused. "What are you doing?"

"I'm shaking the mouse so he won't bite me!"

"He won't bite you. Stop—you'll hurt him."

"I can't. Seth, will you do something!"

"Throw him in the middle of my bed, and I'll grab him."

She lowered her shaking hands, and I got ready to pounce. "Are you ready?"

"Go ahead. Throw him! Easy!"

She tossed him onto the bed. He was so shaken up and dizzy he just lay on the sheet trying to figure out where he was.

"He looks like he's been on a three-week drunk."

I picked him up gently, and watched Mother collapse onto the floor, but she was smiling. Then we were laughing. When we were done, she stood up. "Now you can go to the science fair, and we can all get some sleep. But please take that mouse out to the garage."

After I put him in his cage, I went to Mother's room.

"Is everything all right, Seth?"

"Yes. I just wanted to thank you."

"That's okay, son, you go on to bed now."

"Weren't you afraid of the mouse?"

"Yes, I hate to touch them, but it all turned out all right. He didn't bite me."

"How did you do it?"

"I don't know. I really didn't think about it."

I wondered what she would say about my fears.

"You'd better go to bed now—there's school tomorrow."

"Mother, there are some hoods in school that keep trying to get me to fight. They were the ones who hurt the mouse in the first place."

"Why didn't you tell me before?"

"It's not the kind of thing you tell your mother. You want to handle it yourself, or you still feel like a little kid."

"Do you fight back, Seth?"

"I don't know how."

"Do you want to learn?"

"Would you want me to? Mark's mother is letting him."

"If you fought and won, I'd have to live knowing that my son hurt someone else, that he had to use violence to solve a problem. If you lost, I'd have to live with your pain and watch you trying to be better or tougher so you wouldn't lose the next time. Not a very pleasant choice, is it?"

"I'm sorry."

"I don't want you to learn to fight, Seth, but if you need to defend yourself, I'll find someone to teach you."

"You wouldn't feel good about it."

"There's a third choice. You can try to live with it knowing it won't last forever."

"You mean just endure it?"

"That's a good word for it."

"It means I go to school afraid every day."

"It might mean that for a while."

"If you loved somebody enough, not the people who were hurting you but somebody else, if you loved them enough would the fear finally go away?"

"You're asking a hard question. Fear is very strong. The love would have to be stronger. But I think you love someone that much, Seth. We haven't talked much about it. Some things can't be shared. They need time to rest inside you—but trust in that love and in mine."

"I'll try."

"Will you tell me what happens with fighting?"

"If I can."

"That's good enough. You'd better go to bed now."

The next afternoon, I went to shop. The boy who always demanded the nickels wasn't there. Before we started class, the teacher said, "One of you isn't here today. He'll never set foot in this school again. He was expelled this morning for lighting the fire. I hope this serves as a lesson to you. Now get to work, and no more trouble."

The hoods slid off their workbenches and gathered in a tight knot of malcontent. I could feel them looking at me from time to time. The brassy taste returned to my mouth. Almost instinctively I reached into my pocket to feel the warm sides of the nickel, but it wasn't there. I had been so excited about finding the mouse and so late getting up that I had forgotten it. I searched every pocket twice.

They broke up their group, and one of them came over to my bench. His face was grave, carrying the sum total of all their hate, full, ultimate, and malignant.

"Where's the nickel?"

"I forgot it this morning. I'll bring two tomorrow."

"You didn't forget it. You didn't think you'd need it because you knew Lance wouldn't be here today. You squealed. We're going to get you."

He punched me hard in the back with a force that spun me around and brought tears to my eyes. I blinked them back in a vain effort to control my rising fear.

"I didn't tell a soul. I didn't even know he set the fire. I didn't see him."

"Shut up! We figured it all out. You thought you could get even. You're the only one who would have told."

"I didn't tell. I didn't say a word to anyone."

"Then who did?"

"I don't know."

"Nobody else would tell but you, and we're going to make you pay for it after class."

"But I didn't tell!"

"Sure you didn't. Tell it to the teacher."

He broke my project over the bench, then turned to where the others were waiting.

They stared at me during the rest of the class period, pounding their fists slowly, methodically, into the palms of their hands. I could hear the dull thud they made. Then the shaking began—a slow, steady, hard shaking that grew from all my imagined horrors.

They saw me looking at the clock. One of them slipped over and moved the hands forward ten minutes.

"I didn't tell!" I almost screamed it at him.

"It doesn't matter if you did or not, when that bell rings you're dead."

Help me! I pleaded silently. *They're going to beat me up in a few minutes, and I haven't got anyone to turn to. I've tried to love, but the fear is still there. Please! Please help me!*

I waited to feel the silent reassurance, but nothing came. The bell rang.

They filed out of the door, gathering around, waiting for me to come out. I looked with one last desperate appeal to the teacher, who had retired to his office and was closing the door. He knew what was going to happen and didn't care. He had been through too much.

"Come out and get what's coming to you. He won't help you."

Father, I can't go. I still hate them. I'm afraid.

I took a step toward the door, remembering Mother's words. I took another step. The smiling faces pushed closer, and fear pulled every part of my body into one strangling knot.

When I saw the first fist coming, I threw up my hands to shield my head, but nothing happened. I looked through my hands. One of the boys was standing in front of me, his outstretched hand holding the closed fist of my first attacker. He was one who had never spoken to me.

"Nobody's going to hit him."

"Get out of the way, Joey. Are you crazy?"

"You heard me. We're not going to touch him."

"Come on, Joey."

"You're not going to touch him."

"Joey, get out of my way." It was the boy who spit the Coke and to whom I always paid my nickels. He grabbed Joey's arm and pushed him back. Joey's fist blurred through the air and landed with a thud, sending the boy back into the circle.

"He wasn't the one."

"How do you know?" one of the boys asked.

"He wasn't the one." He stood with his feet apart, his fists closed, sullen and indomitable. They paused for a moment, then one by one turned and walked away.

When they were all gone, he faced me. I was still afraid of him. "You can go home."

I never thanked him. I realized later that I had once played baseball with him in elementary school, but that was all.

I walked across the parking lot to where Mark was waiting.

"Are you all right, Seth? You look kind of funny."

"Yes, I'm all right."

"Those hoods bothering you?"

I told him what happened.

"You were lucky, Seth. What happens when there's no Joey?"

"It wasn't Joey."

"I know what you think, but—"

"It won't make any difference."

He was quiet for a few seconds, then stopped me on the sidewalk. "How do you do it?"

"I don't know, Mark. I just call. He's always there."

"You hear Him speak to you?"

"Not like that. It feels like my own thoughts, only they're His thoughts."

"You're different, Seth. I can't live that way. I pray and everything, but—you know."

We turned the corner in silence and arrived at my front porch. "Mark, are you still going for your Eagle?"

"I guess I'll have to. I told my mother I would."

"We only have a few more months."

"I know. I'll get it. I can't talk about it now. I'm meeting someone."

A motorcycle lurched to a stop next to him, and he climbed on. I watched them slip down the street, out of sight, realizing our roads were separating.

13

A Part of Me

The school year ended, bringing with it the two trophies I coveted most—an Eagle Scout award and the straight "A" report card I promised Mother and Grandpa I'd get the spring I gave up baseball. Mark and I received our Eagle Scouts together, but after that we didn't see much of each other, just at church and occasionally at MIA. No one pushed him around anymore. He assured me of that one night after MIA.

"I got even, Seth. One of them started to push me around and I fought him. I broke his nose. They're nothing but talk when you stand up to them."

"You're different since you started being tough."

"Well, it's better than getting beat up, isn't it? What are you doing this summer?"

"I guess I'll go out to the ranch again."

"I thought you changed your mind."

"What made you think that?"

"You've usually left by now, so I thought that maybe you were staying home this summer."

"There's somebody out there I don't want to see."

"That girl you told me about?"

"That's the reason."

"I thought you liked her."

"Look at me."

"So?"

"She was taller than I was last summer. I don't want to wreck a good memory."

Mark moved to a new ward across town that fall, which ended our relationship. I went into a shell for the next two years. I had fallen down when I was six and cracked part of my jaw. Through the years the bones did not knit together right. The doctor said we needed to fix it. I woke up after the operation and stared into my mother's face.

"Are you awake enough to understand me?"

"I think so. Everything is fuzzy, but I'm all right."

"You're going to need more operations." She looked at the foot of the bed, then the walls.

"How many?"

"There was more damage to the jaw than the X-ray showed. You're going to lose your teeth in front on the right side. You'll have to wear braces to straighten the jaw and the other teeth, but the pressure will be too great for a bridge."

It took weeks, but I learned to talk, smile, and even laugh without showing my teeth. The braces helped. I could catch the inside of my lips on the wires and hold them over my teeth.

I met three other friends during those two years. Cory and Shawn were important at school. My association with them gave me an acceptable position in the social pecking order. The third person was the closest I ever had to a brother. His name was Andy.

Andy was one joke after another. He never stopped smiling, which overly made up for my own sealed lips. We would have made good models for the Greek comedy-tragedy masks. He had black curly hair, olive skin, and a Roman nose. Andy bounced from hobby to hobby.

When I first made friends with him, he was learning taxidermy. He practiced on pigeons he shot with his pellet gun. When his interest in taxidermy died, he turned his attention to model airplane flying, which soon outgrew his pocketbook, as he crashed more than he flew.

Andy could always think of something to do. All of his ideas were crazy. He bought a pair of size fourteen, white arctic snow boots from the army surplus and wore them to school in the heat of September. It started a fad, and soon half the school was clomping down the halls wearing white arctic boots. He went to a stake dance once, dressed as a girl to see if anyone would notice—no one did. He persuaded his dad to buy him an old car. He removed both seats and replaced them. A toilet with pink fur lining became the driver's seat. The passenger side was equipped with a captain's chair on rollers that ran in a foot-long metal track bolted to the floor. When he stepped on the gas, the seat slammed backward. When he braked, which he often did, you thought you were going through the windshield. The back seat was a hammock, also purchased from the army surplus store.

Cory and Shawn were not as colorful, but then neither one needed to be crazy. Shawn was an all-around athlete who bleached his hair blond when he entered high school. Cory was a ladies' man. He had the face of Apollo, the personality of Will Rogers, and the generosity of a corporate president looking for a tax break. You liked Cory from his first hello. He had two great interests besides girls—astronomy and South American archaeology. Cory never drank pop in cans. "It tastes like the inside of an old refrigerator," he told me. "You have to drink pop in a glass with three ice cubes to clink against the sides." I never drank pop in cans again.

Shawn led me around the high school campus that first day I stumbled upon the blacks in the H building restroom. He explained the high school's unwritten rules that everyone was expected to follow.

"You went into the wrong building, Seth. Didn't anyone ever tell you about the buildings?"

"I thought you could go anywhere."

"You can during classes if you have to, but not into the restrooms or lockers."

"Why?"

"It's not our territory. You need to get a locker in the S building. I'll share my locker with you."

"What happens if your locker is in the wrong building?"

"You're in their territory. They wait for you after school and force you out or make you pay protection money. Somebody told me a kid got stabbed a few years ago because he wouldn't change his locker. It's probably just a rumor, but I'm not taking any chances. So bring your books to my locker."

I could feel the old fears beginning to rise. I wondered if I was ever going to be able to go to school without that brassy taint in my mouth.

"The B building belongs to the Mexicans. You shouldn't have to go there until your senior year. Then you'll want to take typing, but you'll be older. If you need to walk through any out-of-bound buildings before or after school, make sure you have a few friends with you or make friends with a black guy or a Mexican and walk with him. Some of them are okay."

"I don't believe this. You're just trying to scare me."

"You still believe that after seeing those guys in the H building bathroom?"

"I guess you're right."

"Also, go right home after school and don't cross the football field or use the back parking lot."

"Why doesn't someone do something about all of this?"

"What can anybody do? That's just the way it is. And don't eat anywhere but in the quad between the S and H buildings and the tables by the machines."

"I thought you said the H building was black?"

"It is, but during lunch we eat in the quad area. They stay by the steps between the H building and the cafeteria."

"You know, Shawn, it feels weird."

"What?"

"To be hated by somebody you don't even know, like those guys in the restroom. Why would somebody want to hurt you when you don't even know them and have never done anything to them?"

"Down in L.A. I've heard it's even worse. You just have to get used to it. They're not all that way, there are a few who mix, but most everybody stays with their own groups."

"Are you going to tell me which classes to switch?"

"Let me see your schedule."

I gave it to him.

"There're only two you need to change."

I rearranged my schedule according to Shawn's instructions and took it in to see the principal. He wouldn't let me make the changes, so I went to my counselor. She was an old friend of my mother's.

"Why do you want to change these classes, Seth?"

"Is it a big deal to change classes?"

"Tell me the truth."

"Because they will be all white."

"That's what I thought. You're contributing to the segregation of the school by asking for this. You know that, don't you?"

"I know."

"You're a Mormon, aren't you?"

"Yes, ma'am."

"Does your church teach you to be prejudiced?"

"No, ma'am."

"Then why are you asking for changes? We will never solve the race problem at this school if everyone does what you're doing."

"I hated junior high school, Mrs. Andrews, because I was afraid of getting beat up. I don't want to go through three more years of that.

"You think this will solve it?"

"No, but at least I can study in peace."

"Would your mother want me to do this for you?"

"My mother would be disappointed in me if she knew, but I walked into the H building bathroom and had a knife pulled on me."

"Why didn't you report it?"

"They were only trying to scare me, and if I reported it, it would be suicide."

"Can't you see that in a mixed classroom the races might find some understanding so those things won't happen?"

"I can see that, Mrs. Andrews, and I feel bad, but I still want the changes."

"Okay. I'll give you your changes on these conditions. I'll make your schedule up every semester. I'll give you classes and a locker in the S building, but I'll give you the hardest classes and the toughest teachers in the school, and they'll make you work. You must maintain a 3.85 average. As long as you do that, I'll keep you in the safe classes."

"Mrs. Andrews, I'm not prejudiced. I don't hate Mexicans and blacks. I just want to be left alone. I'll take your deal if you won't think I'm the worst person in the world because of it."

"I don't think that, Seth. I think very highly of you and your mother and your religion. Maybe that's why I expected more from you. Everyone wants to be left alone. As long as we feel that way we'll have segregation no matter what anyone does, and the problem will get worse. Here's your changed schedule."

I didn't go into the H or B buildings. I followed all the unwritten rules and stayed out of trouble.

I had formed an acquaintance with a boy named Larry during P.E. He approached me one day after class and whispered, "There's going to be a fight in a few minutes by the stadium."

"Who with?" I asked.

"I don't know, but it's going to be a big one, because a whole gang of blacks are hanging around by the fence."

"A white kid's going to fight?"

"Yes. This is a big one! Come on!"

I rushed with him out across the football field, filled with curiosity. We reached the goalposts and I stopped, pulling Larry's arm and pointing to the black students gathering about a hundred feet away.

"You're right. I guess this is far enough."

A group of white boys climbed out of a car and jumped the fence. A couple of them wore white T-shirts and blue tanker jackets. One of them looked vaguely familiar, but he was turned away from me. A white boy stepped out of the group and faced a big black with a blue bandana tied around his head. He spit at the black, and they began to fight, beating each other with a ferocity I had never before seen. Kids were running from all over now, white and black, all of us compelled by an alien sensation that found pleasure in the sight of two creatures fighting.

"Look at them go! You ever see a fight like this, Seth?"

"Not this bad. A friend of mine got beat up once, but not this bad."

Seth, walk away.

I want to see it.

"Come on! Break open!" It was Larry's voice, hot and breathless. "It will break any second now. The coach will never make it."

I turned to see Shawn standing next to me.

"How did you get out of class?"

"I ditched. I've got some friends in there."

Then it broke wide open, seconds before the coach arrived. One of the white boys jumped in to help his friend on the ground, and the next second more than twenty boys were fighting. They all had something in their hands.

Seth, walk away.

Shawn's here. He'll think I'm crazy.

A boy in a blue tanker jacket fell when his head was struck with a board. It was Mark. Then Shawn ran across the field into the fight. He hit a black on the side of the head, but two others pulled him off, threw him to the ground, and kicked him as he went down.

"Look at them go! I told you there would be a big fight. My brother told me about these."

A few more fell, holding their heads and arms. They were kicking Shawn, and Mark hadn't moved. Blood drained out of my head.

"I feel sick, Larry."

"You kidding?"

My hands were wrapped tightly around my middle.

"You going to leave?"

"No. I'll wait till it's over."

I lowered my head, now heavy with my pulse. The voice came again. *You are a part of it.*

Sirens cried in the distance. The fights broke up one by one. I ran across the football field with everyone else. I met Cory at my locker a few minutes later.

"Did you see the fight?"

"I was there."

"I missed it. Tell me about it."

I looked at the eagerness of his eyes. *He's a part of it too*, I thought, *can't help but be a part of it. We are raised with it, maybe even born with it.*

"It's all over now, the police came," I said.

"Well, what happened? Who got hurt?"

"I didn't watch it all. I left when the sirens started."

"You left?"

"Shawn was there. Some black guys were kicking him. I couldn't watch it."

"I wish I'd been there. They don't get big like that very often. Anybody get hurt?"

"Cory, I'm already late for class."

"Tell me the rest."

"Not now. I've got to run."

"Yeah, sure. Catch you after school."

I couldn't stop thinking about the fight. It kept coming back.

When I got home after school, I dialed Mark's number to find out if he was all right. I heard the phone ringing but hung up. I hadn't talked to Mark in months. If his mother answered, I wouldn't have known what to say.

At eight I left my unfinished homework on the desk and stepped outside into the twilight. I climbed a little hill just behind our house where I often went to be alone and found the little clump of brush I usually sat under. I sat for over an hour watching the lights blinking below me.

What have you learned, Seth?

It was always the first question. I thought for a long time.

"There is something inside me, maybe inside us all. It enjoyed what I saw today. I enjoyed it. It's me. Not Satan, but a part of me!"

It can take you to greater dangers.

"Why couldn't I leave even when I was sick? When I'm alone with you here, I know I can overcome anything, but . . ."

I am where men take me.

I looked across the lights of the city far into the distance where they merged with the stars, and I thought of the people living within those lights who struggled against themselves.

I am where men take me.

I nodded, feeling the wind fan my face. It stirred the bushes behind me and bent the long blades of grass over my legs where I knelt. I pushed my fists into my eyes, ashamed of the tears, but the memory returned, the smell of the flooded garden and the bent form of my grandfather. I remembered his words: "Children are wrong about grownups. Don't ever try to hold back tears, Seth, when it's right to cry. You'll know you're becoming a man when you are no longer ashamed of them."

Below me the lights of the city blinked hesitantly. I descended the hill feeling the stale, warm air rising to meet me, hoping desperately that I was carrying the weight.

Everyone was talking about the fight the next day at school, and the lines between the buildings were even more real. Shawn was back even though he had been hurt. Overnight he and others had become heros. He showed up at school with a bruised face and bandaged ribs. They were his medals, and he wore them like a soldier.

"Your friend is a big man today. Some of the other kids got expelled." It was Larry. "Their parents will get them back in a day or two. It was the blacks' fault."

"Larry, how come it's always the blacks' fault?"

"It just always is."

"For us it's always the blacks' fault. It's more convenient that way."

"What're you so angry about?"

"I don't know. Maybe we shouldn't have gone to see the fight."

"Why not? We didn't get hurt, and they can't expel you for watching."

"I know that, but maybe it was wrong."

"To watch a fight?"

"Not just to watch it, but to enjoy it."

"What's wrong with that?"

"Didn't you feel guilty just standing there watching all those boys get hurt?"

"Are you Mormons nonviolent?"

"No."

Shawn saw me talking to Larry and came down the hallway.

"Where did you go yesterday?" he asked. "I looked for you after the police left."

"He thinks it's wrong to watch fights. It's part of his religion."

"It's not part of his church. I'm a Mormon too."

"There, see, your own members don't agree with you."

"All I'm saying is I don't think it's good to enjoy watching two kids beating each other up. I felt guilty, that's all."

They were both looking at me now. Larry had even stopped eating, then he stuffed the last of his sandwich into his mouth and muttered, "Maybe you're right, but it's not going to change anything."

Mark came back to school three days later. I had been watching for him, wondering if he had been expelled or was in the hospital. He had a bruise on the side of his head, but other than that no one could tell he was any different, but I knew. He was building a wall. It was the first wall I recognized on anyone other than my father, and I wondered how much he was hiding behind it.

"You all right, Mark?"

"Yeah."

"I heard you were in the hospital."

"Rumors. I stayed in bed at home so I wouldn't get expelled."

"I wanted to call."

"I wondered if you would. I saw you standing on the field."

"I didn't know what to say to your mother, so I hung up."

"I don't blame you. She was pretty upset. I'm not turning out to be the ideal Mormon boy."

"None of us are."

"What have you ever done wrong?"

"I haven't done all the right things either."

"Not you. You're the one that feels the voices, remember? You still have those things?"

"Sometimes. Mark, why don't you drop those friends?"

"They're not really friends, just some guys I hang around with. I've got a girlfriend now."

"That's great."

"You still like that girl in Nevada?"

"I've never seen her again."

"Too bad. I'd better get going." He started to go, then turned. "Listen, Seth. Things can be rougher in high school than junior high, especially with the blacks, so if you ever need anyone—I mean, you know who to ask.

"I'll remember, Mark. Come over sometime, okay?"

I watched his hunched-over figure disappearing down the corridor.

14

Behind the Wall

Summer once again brought the hot, carefree days of the ranch and Utah. I spent a little time at each place, cutting my trip to Utah short because Grandpa was depressed. His oldest son, Lars, Grandpa's pride, had requested that his name be taken off the Church records. Grandpa believed he would never come back.

I sat one evening on the patio and listened to Grandpa talk to my mother. His voice was weaker now, beaten, and filled with a sadness that was a wall in itself. For the first time in my life I thought of him as an old man.

"Look what happened to me, Daddy," my mother said. "Did you ever give up hope with me?"

"You were young and rebellious. Lars is a grown man with a family."

"I was an adult with two children."

"You started when you were young and didn't know any better."

"Maybe he did too, Daddy."

He shifted in his chair and looked across the lawn to the darkness where the garden lay. "Why did you rebel?"

"Now's not the time, Daddy. You'll just blame yourself more."

He leaned up from his chair and spoke with force, searching my mother's face. "There never will be a time."

She began cautiously, watching his face until it got too dark to see his features, and her words came easier. "Everything you did was so serious. There were too many lessons and not enough laughter."

"They were hard times."

"Hard for us, too. We didn't know how you felt. We knew your beliefs, your faith, not you. We worried about pleasing you and being accepted."

"I wanted you to know the temptations and how to be strong."

"We knew them, Daddy. You warned us, but you never showed us the joy or the love. God was always like you in my eyes, righteous but distant."

"I wanted you to think I was strong."

"I thought you were strong. We all did. You never had a weakness in my eyes. I had too many. I was afraid to come to you with my own."

"You rebelled—against me?"

"Not against you, against the gospel."

"Jens and Lars were like you?"

"Jens tried so hard to please you. He did everything you did. You never told him how proud you were of him."

"But I was proud, of both of them."

"They never knew. Jens kept struggling, trying harder and harder. Daddy, I'm hurting you, let's stop."

"I need to know how my children feel. I need to know what I've done to them."

"But you've learned. You've become a father to my son. You've shared your life with him. All the stories that mean so much to him now would have meant a lot to us. I typed your story for myself, too. It came too late for me, but not too late for him."

"It doesn't matter now."

"Life is for learning, Daddy. If God worried about my whole life with all its failures and not what it's taught me, not what I've become, then there is no hope for me."

"Why did you come back?"

"Because my husband had weaknesses but was trying to live the gospel, and because that first night I prayed, God told me that all of life was for perfection, not just the first half of it."

They both stopped talking for what seemed minutes. Grandpa rubbed his hands back and forth across the thin material at his knees where he worked in the garden.

"Daddy? Are you all right?"

He didn't answer for a long while. "It's hard for a father to lose his sons."

"One person never carries all the blame. Put them out of your mind for now."

He couldn't put them out of his mind. Mother, sensing that he wanted to be left alone, packed the car, and we left for California. The last day there we saw my father again. He was not taking us to Lagoon anymore—now it was dinner at a fancy restaurant. His hair was graying, and he looked older. The smell of his aftershave was still too strong. I hadn't seen him for several years, but all the little details came back— the tapping ring, the tight lips, Jan's nervousness, and the eyes that never focused on me.

"I haven't seen you for a few years, Seth. Just the pictures your Mother sent."

"I haven't changed much."

"Your mother tells me you're quite a scholar."

"I've been lucky."

"Are you going to college?"

"I'm saving for it."

"Yes, I know."

"A lot of it's your money. I've never said thank you."

He took a drink from the water glass and straightened the silverware.

"I expect you'll get a scholarship."

"Then I'll use the money for a mission."

"That would be lovely. You spend all summer at the ranch?"

"Yes."

"Do you like it out there?"

"I can't think of another place I'd rather be."

"Your Uncle Morgan is a great man. I've always liked him."

"You know Uncle Morgan?"

"I've talked with him a few times."

"When?"

"During the past years."

"About what?"

"Nothing very important, just talk. Why didn't you stay out there this summer?"

"Mother wanted me to come to Utah to see Grandpa. He's depressed about Lars. Mother thought if I worked in the garden with him he'd feel better, but it didn't work."

"It must be terrible for him. He loved Lars very much."

"Lars won't even see him."

"That's the saddest of all." He took another drink and stared at my forehead.

We left the next morning. I sat in the front seat with Mother while my sisters slept in the back. She noticed me staring out the window.

"What are you thinking about?" she asked.

"Grandpa."

"Just Grandpa?"

"And Mark and my father."

"Mark?"

"Mark's eyes are like his. They don't really look at you. They're like a wall with something hiding behind them."

"And Grandpa?"

"I always thought the things behind people's walls were bad things. I know some of the things Mark has done, but now Grandpa has a wall too, like he did when Uncle Jens died, but Grandpa's not hiding anything, is he?"

"No, he has nothing to hide, but he's very sad."

"Maybe the walls just hide sadness."

"All walls aren't built with sins, Seth, or broken commandments. Sometimes they're built of lost opportunities and might-have-beens."

"And behind the wall there is nothing?"

"Only emptiness and sorrow."

15

An Open Door

We returned to California, where I spent the rest of the summer on the beach with Andy and Shawn. Shawn was into surfing now. I could never get the hang of it. I got tired of chasing the board every time a wave hit, so I spent the days body surfing with Andy. When we weren't in the water, Andy was playing his guitar and trying to teach me the chords to Beach Boys songs. It was his newest passion. I bought a cheap guitar and joined him. By summer's end I had learned to play enough songs from the radio to cover the sixty-minute drive to the ocean. Most of the time Mother drove us down and sat on the beach. She treated my friends just as she treated me, and they all loved her.

When we were in the water, Andy and Shawn talked about girls. They were dating. Shawn already had a steady girlfriend, and if Andy could have had his fondest wish he'd have had one too. My braces weren't off yet, and I still had an ugly space in my teeth. Both problems gave me a good excuse for not joining them. I could feel their excitement, though, and I was envious.

"When school starts again, Seth, we'll double."

"I won't be sixteen."

"I'm not sixteen."

"Your parents let you. My mother is sticking to sixteen, and I promised my uncle. Besides, nobody will go out with me till I get these teeth fixed."

"You worry about them too much. I've seen girls dance with you at the stake dances."

"They have to there. Going out is different. I'll wait till I can smile."

"Who are you going to ask out for your first date?"

"I haven't decided yet. I guess I'll have to race some mice."

"Mice?"

"It's a family joke."

"You know what I think? I think you like having those braces. It gives you an excuse to avoid girls."

"Most of them can rest their chin on my head."

"That's another excuse. What about that girl in Nevada? She was taller than you."

"So?"

"You still carry that arrowhead in your wallet?"

"I took it out last year."

"She liked you."

"She felt sorry for me. Something happened that was hard on me. She must have guessed how I felt about it."

Shawn swam over to us, pushing his surfboard. "Anyone want to try it?"

"Shawn's joining the frat this year." Andy jumped on the surfboard as he said it. Shawn dumped him off.

"You're not really, are you, Shawn?"

"Most of my friends are rushing it in the fall."

"But the frat—"

"Those are rumors. Most of the guys are really good."

"The girls like frat boys," Andy said. "Cory's rushing, too."

"How do you know that?" I asked.

"He told me last week," Shawn said. "He won't have any trouble because his brother belonged when he was in high school."

"Cory is a real ladies' man," Andy responded. "It fits him."

I looked back at Shawn. "Is your Dad going to let you join the frat?"

"He doesn't care as long as I keep my grades up, and it doesn't bother my basketball."

"But Shawn, the frat!"

"I told you they were just rumors. You don't know. Have you ever been to one of their parties? Cory's brother told us about them. They get wound up sometimes, but he always left. Besides, most of the student government and guys on the team belong. I'm in both, so I have a responsibility."

Sixteen came quickly. In January the dentist put a bridge into place. Finally I had a smile and confidence I hadn't felt for years. The first few days I smiled at every stray dog on the sidewalk, but that finally wore off. Andy was at me immediately to double with him. I settled down to the serious business of whom to ask out for my first date.

"Who's it going to be?" Andy asked me one day.

"How about Linda?"

"Won't work. She's the kind of girl whose guppies are going to have babies the night the wrong boy asks her out."

"How about Chris?"

"Is she the one that dances with you at the stake dances?"

"That's Chris."

"She's not bad looking. Ask her."

"What are we going to take them to?"

"There's a concert in the auditorium. It's the easiest thing to go to. You're spared the agony of wondering what to say—you just watch the concert. We'll treat them to a milkshake and take them home."

"I'm still nervous."

"You're scared to death, but we'll have a great time. Just act like a gentleman. It always works—then you can kiss her goodnight on the doorstep."

"This is the first time I'm taking her out."

"She'll let you. Picture yourself on the front doorstep with her after the concert. Makes your heart beat faster, doesn't it?

"I'd be scared spitless!"

"You're excited just thinking about it. All right, I'll tell you how. You just put your hands on her arms like this and kiss her. Then see how long you can make it last."

"I don't think I should on a first date."

"You've danced with her at the dances, so it's not like a first date."

"Maybe."

"I think you're weakening. You've wanted to from the beginning."

"Well, everyone wants to kiss a girl. You're not normal if you don't want to."

"If you do, I'll treat you to the biggest shake in town. If you don't, you treat me." He held out his hand expectantly. I took it.

"Okay, I'll kiss her goodnight."

"Now you're talking. A long one?"

"You didn't say anything about how long it had to be."

"As long as mine?"

"You take your date home first so I can watch."

I worried about that last moment a hundred times, trying to decide exactly the right way to do it and wondering if I would really go through with it.

The night finally came. I picked up Andy. We drove to pick up our dates. I stepped out of the car. Andy grabbed my arm and whispered, "You still going through with it?"

"I will if you will."

Chris came to the door and took my arm. Her hand was warm. "Thanks for asking me, Seth."

She squeezed my arm. I didn't need Andy's prodding anymore. I couldn't wait for the date to end. The concert dragged on and on. The only bright spots were the knowing glances Andy kept passing my way. Halfway through the concert I wiped my hands on my pantlegs and slowly took Chris's hand. Her fingers closed around mine.

Andy and I waited in the lobby after the concert for the girls to come out of the restroom. "How come they always go in the restroom, Andy? This is the third time."

"They're hoping for the doorstep too. They don't want any stray hairs out of place."

"I don't think that's why."

"You doubt me? You won't have any trouble at the doorstep if you move slow enough and act confident. Take her hand again when they come out."

We took them to 31 Flavors and bought them a milkshake. Then we drove to where Andy's date lived. He walked her to the door with his arm around her shoulder. He talked with her for what seemed an eternity. I felt conspicuous sitting next to Chris. I tried to talk to her and watch Andy at the same time. I did a lousy job. She noticed my glances toward the doorway.

"You can watch them if you want to, Seth. I'd like to watch, too." She smiled while she said it.

"What's he waiting for?" she said a few seconds later.

"I think he's moving slow and gaining confidence." I laughed nervously.

Finally he kissed her. I counted the seconds until they reached an unbelievable six.

Chris whistled softly. "He's not bad for an amateur!"

Andy hurried back to the car, giving me an exultant look as he climbed into the back seat. I could see him puckering his lips at me through the rearview mirror. I pulled into Chris's driveway, deliberately stopping the car behind the front trees to make Andy's view of the front porch obscure.

I circled around and opened the door for her. The porch light was on, highlighting her face and cheeks. Just like in the movies, I thought. Under its glow she was the best-looking girl I had ever seen.

I kept thinking, "Slow and confident."

She looked at me and smiled, then thanked me for the evening. In the back of my mind I could see Andy hunched up over the front seat trying to watch. I moved her a little so she couldn't see the car. All thoughts of bets were gone. The feeling was stronger than the hundred times I had imagined this moment during the last week. I took her arms in my hands, leaned forward, and kissed her. I was off center. I tried to straighten it out, which didn't work very well. I could feel her lips twist into a smile.

I didn't count the seconds. I just let the feeling, off center or not, carry me on, leaving me a little breathless and wishing I had kept it up a little longer.

"Thanks for a lovely evening, Seth. Will you be at the next stake dance?"

"Yes."

"Was I all right for a first date?"

"Great!" It came out with too much enthusiasm. She smiled a last time and closed the door. I turned to see Andy bouncing out of the back seat of the car and rushing to the driver's door. He opened it for me with a flourish.

"Let me be the first to open the door for a real man!"

I jumped at that word. Andy noticed immediately.

"Hey, what's the matter? What did I say?"

He circled the front of the car and climbed into the front seat. A memory surfaced. I felt a breeze fanning my face.

"Didn't you like it, Seth?"

I nodded.

"Well, if you liked it how come you look so serious all of a sudden?"

"I'm sorry, Andy. I just remembered something."

"It must have been pretty big."

"It's nothing. When are we going on our next date?"

"Are you going to take Chris out again?"

"I guess so. Maybe I should ask another girl."

"Ask Chris. You'll have to start all over with another girl. Picture Chris on the front porch, smiling, waiting for you."

"Yeah, maybe."

"We'll go up in the mountains next time. There's a waterfall I know about."

"Sure, Andy."

I took Andy to his house and drove home in the darkness. I was too tired to settle it in my mind. I was still excited. I'd work it out in the morning.

Morning came. I couldn't admit to Him that I was wrong. I was still confused. The remembrance was exhilarating. After the two-year toothless famine, it seemed too good to be true. I felt proud at school when Andy talked to Shawn and Cory.

A few days later I went to a school club meeting with Cory. I had borrowed Mother's car and promised her I'd be home a little after the meeting let out. When it ended I brought the car around and waited for Cory.

"Pull around to the back stairs and wait for me there. I've got to talk to someone," he shouted.

When I pulled to a stop at the back stairs and honked, Cory came out of the building with two girls. "They need a ride home, Seth. Can you give them a lift?"

"Sure. Just tell me where you live."

Cory opened the back door and helped one of the girls in, sliding next to her as he entered. The other girl opened the front door and climbed in next to me.

I looked at the girl sitting on the front seat. She had shoulder length blond hair that curled under her chin. She was in the tenth grade, shorter and younger than me. She was even better looking than Chris.

"Seth, meet Susan. And this is Janet." Cory put his arm around the girl in the back seat.

"Where do you live?" I asked.

She smiled at me and put her arm on the back of my seat.

"Just go down Elm. I'll tell you when to turn."

I drove down the street a few minutes listening to them talk.

"Why don't we cruise Baseline?" Cory suggested.

His suggestion met with quick approval from the girls.

"I've never seen much sense in cruising, Cory," I said half-heartedly.

"Come on. Everyone does it."

"Haven't you ever cruised?" Susan asked.

"I know how, I just promised to get the car home."

"Your mother won't care. She takes us everywhere," Cory said. "Besides, we got out early. We have time for a few runs."

Susan's eyes were on me. I didn't have the courage to look back. She stared so long I became uncomfortable.

"Come on, Seth. It'll be fun. Then we can go right home."

She said it in a semi-whisper. I finally turned to look at her. She had that same smile I had seen on Chris's face a few nights before. She turned on the radio and moved a little closer.

I swung the car around and started down Baseline, feeling a little guilty at first and hoping no one would see me. Eventually I loosened up with the music and the talk. After the first run Cory was quiet in the back seat. I hadn't looked back at him for some time. We were coming up Baseline for the third run when I finally looked in the rearview mirror. Cory was wrapped up in Janet's arms. I shifted my eyes to the road, straightening the car, and glanced into the mirror again. They were still kissing.

Susan was aware of my discovery almost before I was. She bent forward, her eyes smiling. "This is a nice song." She smiled again.

Fists began squeezing my heart, and my mind was racing. The music made the air heavy—impossible to breathe. I could almost swallow the words. I found a voice, but it was weak and lacked conviction.

"Cory, we're at the end of the third run. Maybe we ought to be heading home."

There were a few seconds of hesitation, then a smothered voice came from the back seat. "It's still early, Seth. Let's drive around a little more."

"I promised I'd have the car home early. We'd better go."

"Come on, Seth. Just a little longer."

He leaned over the front seat. I turned to Susan, trying to look past her so I wouldn't have to face that smile.

"Where do you live? I'll take you home first."

I figured that would give Cory the time he needed in the back seat. I turned off Baseline waiting for an answer.

"Do you have to take us home now?" There was just a touch of pity in her voice. She smiled and waited for an answer.

"It's just that it's getting late."

"It's only nine o'clock."

My mind filled with imagination and then a beginning fear.

"Let's go one more time." Her voice was low.

I wanted to give in. And then came Cory's voice, less than a whisper. "Let's drive up to the point."

"Well, it's getting late."

"Haven't you ever been to the point before?" It was Susan now, speaking so softly the notes of the music almost drowned out her voice.

"I've been there."

As a kid I'd thrown firecrackers under the seemingly empty cars and laughed in delight, running down the hill, as the heads jerked into view above the dashboards.

"Kiss him, Susan." Cory settled down into the back seat. Susan slid across the remaining distance, put her hand on my neck, and softly pushed next to me. The weight of her hand was barely noticeable. I turned the car in the direction of the point and wished I was already there so I could turn to her and give in. I tried to cut the last string of resistance the fear kept building. The music poured from the radio.

"Relax a little, Seth. You're all tense," Susan said quietly. I wanted to know what it was like, but I didn't like the other feeling that was filling the car.

"Turn off a little way up the hill. There's a dirt road most people don't know about."

I looked at her. She smiled, then closed her eyes and laid her head on my shoulder.

Softly, piercing, the warning—*These are the greater dangers.*

Then another voice came. *Would you like to know what happened to that bull, Seth? He pushed the door all the way open, and it swung wide to let him pass, but when he turned around to get out, the door swung shut.*

I took my foot off the gas and loosened my grip on the steering wheel. I reached over and turned off the radio, moving her head off my shoulder as I did so. I couldn't look at her. I just looked straight ahead. Cory sat up.

"What's the matter now, Seth?"

I had to get it all out at once, just to clear the atmosphere. "I'm taking you all home."

"Oh, come on, Seth!"

"Please, Cory."

"Are you crazy?"

"Are you going to tell me where they live?"

I put the brakes on and watched with relief as Susan slid across the seat. "Turn around and go back to the school," Susan said. "We'll walk from there."

"I'll drive you home."

"We'll walk."

In silence I drove them back to the school. Then I drove to Cory's house.

"You going to say something, Cory?"

"No."

I turned into his driveway and shut off the car. He started to get out. I tried again.

"Cory, I know you wanted to do me a favor. I just couldn't go through with it."

He slammed the door.

"I don't want to break up our friendship. I'm sorry."

"Then you explain it to me. You made a fool of yourself out there, and I looked like one too. Susan's one of the cutest girls I know, and I lined her up for you. I made sure she was small enough, and even explained to her you were a little new so she'd have to get things going."

"I don't know if I can explain."

"Try! I want to hear it."

He opened the door and slipped into the front seat.

"It was wrong, Cory. I was afraid if I got started I couldn't quit. I shouldn't have kissed Chris when I took her out."

"Oh, come on, Seth, one little kiss at the doorstep?"

"It's not that. I'm afraid of where it might lead."

"You make me feel like a sinner just because I've kissed a few girls for the fun of it."

"I'd feel guilty, Cory. Maybe it's just—"

"Go on."

"I wanted to go and make out at the point tonight with Susan. You don't know how badly I wanted to go, but I felt a fear and a warning I just couldn't go against. I love God. I feel terrible when I disappoint Him."

I looked at Cory. He was fingering the edge of the car seat.

"You don't think God approves of me because I make out?"

"I don't think He wants us to do it unless it means something, not just a thrill to get excited about, so it wouldn't matter who it was as long as she was cute."

"I still don't think it's wrong."

"Cory, when I was at my uncle's ranch in Nevada, I'd get bucked off the horses a lot. My uncle would laugh and say, 'The safest place in the world is the back of a horse, Seth. It's when you get off that the trouble begins.'

"One day we found some missing cows in a little pocket of sagebrush behind a hill. One of them had a bull calf that had never seen a man or horse before. It was over a year old, pretty big and wild. He charged our horses. We had to round up the cows and drive the bull in the middle of them. It was the only way we could work him.

"It took us about four hours to get him back to the ranch. When we got there my uncle said, 'Now Seth, that bull is wilder that you think, so don't get down. Just bend over and unlock the gate from your horse and let the cows go in. The bull should go in with them.'

"The cows came to the corral gate. I rode ahead of them and un-latched the gate. The cows walked right in, but the bull backed away. I chased him a few times, but he wouldn't go. He finally backed himself into a corner by the fence. I tried everything I could think of to get him out, but he just stood there. I decided to climb down and throw some-thing at him. I walked away from my horse a few steps and yelled, but he wouldn't budge, so I picked up a rock the size of a baseball and threw it. It hit him in the soft part of his nose. He shook the pain off for a second then charged out of the corner. I ran for the fence. You know, Cory, as I was running I would have given just about anything to have been back on my horse. Anyway, I jumped as high as I could and barely cleared the top of the fence.

"I don't know if I'm explaining this very well, but I felt like I climbed off my horse tonight and was about to throw rocks at the bull. The feel-ings I had inside me when Susan slid over next to me and you said we were going to the point were so strong I knew somehow they could run me down."

I stopped talking and we sat for a while.

"Cory, why don't you quit the frat?"

"I'll think about it."

"I wish Shawn would, too."

"Don't worry, Seth. I promise I'll think about the frat."

"Okay. It's getting late. I guess your dad will be worried."

"That's okay. Dad's on another business trip, and Mom's working late tonight. Do you want to come in for a while?"

"I'd better get the car home."

He waved to me, just before stepping inside, and turned on the lights. I turned the key and drove home.

I knelt by my bedside and felt His smile and knew again that my grandfather had been right.

"How can You be proud? I wanted to go to the point. I'm afraid, Father. I still want to go to the point. Maybe I'll always want to go to the point, and I'm afraid for Cory. What can I do?"

I knelt, waiting. Then the word filled my mind. *Covenant.*

I bent with His word and felt the trembling inside. "I promise. I will wait until I can give the love with affection, not take it selfishly. I will wait until I can accept the love gratefully and without shame."

I climbed into bed and pulled the blankets around my neck. He was still smiling.

16

Still His Son

I should have known it would be impossible to keep it a secret. Susan was too outraged not to spread it around, so I got the name of "Frog." I had not yet kissed a princess. The name stuck.

"Don't let them get to you," Cory said one day at lunch.

"I'd like to apologize to Susan, try to explain."

"She's not worth it. It'll only make things worse. The year will be over in a few months, and it'll all be forgotten."

"I killed it with Shawn, didn't I?"

"Not really."

"I guess I can't blame him. It's hard to be loyal to the frat and a kid everybody thinks is weird."

"It's just at school. I know he tried to defend you at the last meeting."

"You quit the frat, didn't you?"

"Last week."

"Were they hard on you?"

"I never needed it in the first place. It ruined it for Andy, though.

They were going to let him in."

"Andy? You're kidding."

"They wanted his car."

"He'll never forgive me."

Andy didn't care. One noon, to avoid the catcalls in the quad, he took me out to eat.

"Why don't we go down to Jefferson and watch the first-graders run," he suggested.

"I haven't been back to One-Strap Annie's for years."

"Let's go. We'll be back in time for fifth period and can catch the noon runners."

"I'd sure like to get away from this place."

"I thought you would."

We drove to the elementary school and parked the car by the fence. The same knot of nervous little boys were trying to watch without attracting attention. Under the principal's window a row of cautious figures dashed for the fence leading to the alley.

"Did you touch the wall in first grade, Andy?"

"We lived across town then. My little brother is supposed to run this week, and he's been worried about it for days. I didn't want to take the thrill away from him so I told him she'd turn him into one of her cats if she caught him."

"I know what he feels like."

"You ran as a first grader?"

"Ran and got caught. Some junior-high boys hung me on the wall just as One-Strap was coming. She pulled me in with a rake."

"Then it's true? There is a One-Strap Annie?"

"Every detail, right down to the cats. I was a hero for weeks."

"Can you come over after school today?"

"I guess so. Why?"

"Just a second."

He hopped out of the car and ran to the fence. A second later his little brother emerged from the gaggle of boys. I looked down the alley as a light blond tiger tore down the gravel, hit the wall with his foot, and ran back, his face whiter than powder.

Andy returned to the car. "It's all set. I told my little brother my best friend had actually seen One-Strap Annie. Half the first grade will be at the house just to see you."

"Why did you tell him that? What am I supposed to do with a pack of little boys?"

"I thought you could use some adoration for a change."

"This isn't exactly the type I had in mind."

Three hours later I perpetuated the legend of One-Strap Annie in front of twenty spellbound little boys. From that time on, however, the legend included a rusted rake.

Every semester Larry and I seemed to have a few classes together. One day in English while I was waiting for class to start, he came up behind me and sat down.

"Listen, Seth. I've been giving you a bad time about Susan. I'm sorry. I want to make it up to you."

"You don't have to make up anything, Larry."

"Well, it's all in fun, but I want to do something just to prove there are no hard feelings."

"That's all right, Larry."

"I know you don't like wild girls, so I can line you up with a good friend of mind who thought what you did was pretty neat when Susan put the move on you."

"I don't think I'd—"

"Hear me out. First, I'm not going to stick you, so don't get nervous. Second, you know her. She's tried to hint to you she'd like to go out, but you're too dense to catch on."

"Who is she?"

"She's in your math class."

My mind whirled up and down the rows of faces in my math class.

"There's a big game this weekend—"

"Larry, for crying out loud, who is she?"

"You don't know, do you?"

"Of course I don't know—you won't tell me."

"She's not a Mormon. Is that going to make a difference?"

"It might make a difference," I said, remembering Susan.

"Even if she's not wild?"

"Larry, are you going to tell me who she is?"

"I don't want to arrange this if you're going to shoot her down because she isn't Mormon."

"I'm not going to shoot anyone down because they're not Mormon."

"Are you interested?"

"I'd probably go out with her, Larry, but we'll never find out because you won't tell me who she is!"

Just then Miss Woodall walked in. She was the kind of teacher that started lecturing the minute she walked in the door. She loved literature and kept me spellbound the full fifty minutes as she introduced us to "the great thoughts of man." I liked her better than any other teacher I ever had, even though she permitted absolutely no talking in class.

"Woody's here. Larry, tell me quick," I muttered.

He settled back into his seat just as Miss Woodall started class. A thought grabbed me. Maybe there wasn't a girl, and he had thought the whole thing up. Like a jerk, I'd fallen for it. I turned and whispered. "There isn't any—" I wasn't quick enough.

"Mr. Michaels. Do you have something important to say? I think the whole class ought to hear."

"No, Miss Woodall. I have nothing important to say."

"I got the distinct impression you wanted to say something to Mr. Sloan."

"It can wait till after class."

"No, if it's that important you had better get it taken care of now. Go ahead with your question."

She must have had a bad morning, I thought. Miss Woodall's moods had been classified by past generations of students into three climates, sunny, stormy, and full gale. Every period passed the weather report on to the next. I had seen her give a full gale third degree to other students and had avoided it like the plague all year.

I couldn't think of what to say. I couldn't ask the real question. I knew what would happen if I said, "There isn't any girl, Larry." Why would "The Frog" be concerned with girls? I could hear the teasing already.

"I believe you started out, 'There isn't any . . .' Would you finish your sentence so we can go on with class?"

If I lied, Larry would be on me for being hypocritical.

"Please, Miss Woodall, I'm sorry. It won't happen again."

"I take it your question would prove embarrassing. Next time I won't let you off."

She turned to the board and began her lecture with everyone still a little tense. Larry leaned forward and whispered, "A full gale today. I wonder where she'll strike next."

Halfway through the class, Larry slipped a note to me. I pushed it into the palm of my hand, not daring to look at it for fear Miss Woodall would see. When she turned the next time to write on the board I opened the note and saw the name, Anna Cortes. I had to restrain myself. She was shorter than I was. She was also one of the nicest girls I knew, a foreign exchange student from Spain with a timid smile and black hair that went to her waist. Everyone liked her. She was not overwhelmingly beautiful, but she was attractive. I had spoken to her a few times, but then, she spoke to everyone. The period finally ended and released me from the bondage of silence. I turned to speak to Larry, but Miss Woodall cut me off.

"Mr. Michaels, I'd like to speak to you for a few minutes."

"Yes, ma'am?"

She waited till the room cleared before continuing.

"The English language, Mr. Michaels, is made up of words. Thousands of words. Some people can take those words and arrange them in such a way that you're sure the author is thinking your thoughts and feeling your feelings. It's a gift—one of the most priceless. I'm giving you back your creative writing assignment. Your grade is a "C," not because it's "C" work, but because you have the ability to make words mean more. I'll expect it back next week, and I want those words to sing. I want to feel what you feel. You're not there yet."

"I'll try—"

"Don't try! There's one more thing. I'm recommending you for the Teacher's Association Scholarship. It's a thousand dollars. You won't write an essay until next year, but I want you to start thinking about it now. Here's a list of books I'd like you to read. They'll help you."

"Thank you."

"That's all, then. And Mr. Michaels. The English language was never meant to be degraded into notes passed in a literature class. Remind Mr. Sloan of that."

"Yes, ma'am, I will."

Larry was waiting for me when I walked out the door. "Was it bad?"

"Just stormy."

"Well, what do you say about Anna?"

"She's a nice girl."

"Will you go out with a Catholic?"

"Why do you say things like that?"

"Just kidding. Anyway, do you want to go? There's a car-decorating contest before the game. We'll decorate my car together, then drive down to the game. You don't even need to phone her. I'll make all the arrangements."

"Okay, Larry, talk to her. I'll go with you."

For the rest of the week I tried to avoid seeing Anna. I managed to come a little late to math and stayed after class to talk to the teacher. Andy was in the same class and got on me for it.

"How come you won't talk to her?"

"What if it's a setup? I'll wait until Saturday and see."

"I don't believe you."

"I'm scared. I don't want to blow it again."

"Make a gab list. You know, ten things you can talk about."

"I'm not that desperate."

By Saturday morning I was that desperate. I locked myself in my bedroom and made the list. Behind everything else was the fear. I wasn't anxious to go through that again.

Saturday night brought Larry to my doorstep with fifty yards of crepe paper and a hundred balloons. We drove to the school and picked up Anna and Larry's date. We decorated the car with a relish that helped us past the initial awkwardness. I kept my list in mind, but Anna was easy to talk to. She told me all about Spanish literature. I had read *Don Quixote* in Woody's class, which helped.

At the sound of a whistle, all the cars drove caravan-style with a full police escort down the main street of town. We arrived at the other school's stadium and parked the cars. I took Anna's hand and followed Larry up the stairs.

We had a traditional spring football game to give the seniors one last chance to play. Usually it was the best game of the year. All went well with Anna until halftime. We sat in the card section, where at a given signal certain people held up different colored cards to spell out cheers and cartoons for the opposing side to see. It was traditional for those in the card section to throw their cards as the team came back on the field. A few injuries had led to outlawing card throwing, and the police were watching carefully. The temptation was too great for the students. Every few seconds someone sailed a card over the head of a policeman. The one who threw it sat down quickly, or a whole bleacher section would stand up around him and point to each other. It drove the police crazy, and soon the bleachers were rocking with laughter. Larry threw his card perfectly, then turned to me. Anna was laughing with the rest of the students. I gripped the corner of my card, let go of Anna's hand, glanced at the police, stood up and threw the card out over the field. It went two feet over the head of the policeman, and the bleachers rolled in laughter. I didn't sit down fast enough. The policeman turned just in time to see my head bob down.

"You're caught! He's coming up the stairs," Larry whispered. "He's at the foot of the middle platform, waving for you to come down."

"You sure he's looking at me?"

"Yes, but sit still," Larry said, "and hope for a miracle."

Half the students were aware of what was happening and began to catcall the officer. He signaled again with more authority. I rose and descended the long stairs. I could hear Larry's voice behind me.

"He can't do anything. He doesn't really know you threw it. There were other kids standing."

There were thousands of steps, all lined with faces. When I was face to face with my interrogator, he gripped my shoulder and looked me straight in the eye.

"Did you throw that last card?"

Larry was right—he didn't know I had thrown it. Someone behind me said, "No, he didn't throw it. I saw some other kid do it. Quit picking on the poor guy."

Larry shouted down. "You got the wrong guy. Leave him alone."

I hadn't said anything yet. He gripped me tighter and asked again, "You threw that last card, didn't you?"

I nodded my head. Larry put both hands to his head and slumped back down into his seat.

"Don't I get any consideration for telling the truth?"

"It's funny how kids always say that when they're caught. You're going to get kicked out of the game."

"But I've got a date up there. Couldn't you make an exception this time?"

"You can take her out with you if you want."

I could see it was no use arguing. He was the kind of adult that thought everyone needed to be taught a lesson. I pictured myself walking back up the steps and saying to Anna, "Would you mind sitting in the parking lot with me during the second half of the game?"

"I don't think I'll ask her. I'll go alone."

He pulled me unceremoniously down the steps past the cheerleaders, which added insult to injury, as Susan was one of them, then out the front gate to the parking lot. My one consolation was the round of boos he received as we filed past the bleachers. As we turned the last corner, another card sailed through the air, and I heard the roar of approval that followed its passage. As it hit the ground somebody shouted, "There's a lily pad for you to sit on!"

Not another soul was in the parking lot, just me and the decorated cars dripping crepe paper. A full half of the game was left. It would take me that long to think up what I was going to say to Larry and Anna when it was over.

"Maybe I ought to walk the ten miles home. It'd be easier than facing Anna and Larry," I said to a yellow Volkswagen. I walked around the lot twenty times, cussing my stupidity and listening to the cheers coming from the stadium.

After the game, I climbed into the back seat of Larry's car and pretended to be asleep. Anna tapped on the window. I got out and opened the door for her. All my one-liners fled. All I could think of was my list of ten subjects.

"Were you really asleep?"

"No, just pretending. It was easier that way."

"I'm sorry you missed the last half."

"Not as sorry as I am."

"It was really good, especially the last five minutes."

"Who won?"

"They did, but it was close."

At the school parking lot we discarded the remains of the crepe paper. Anna said, "We'll walk home, Larry—it's just around the corner. Thanks for taking us to the game. Seth, I'm sorry again you got thrown out."

I touched her elbow as she was turning around. "Anna, I'm sorry I messed up the evening for you. I'm sorry I embarrassed you—if I did."

"Oh, don't apologize, Seth. It's just that—"

"It's just that what?"

"It's just that I thought you were different."

She turned and left with her friend. Larry put his hand on my shoulder. "It's my fault, Seth."

"No, it isn't, Larry. You want to drive me home now?"

We drove without talking. Anna's words were still in my mind: "I thought you were different." But I hadn't lied, and I could have. Didn't that count? I was so wrapped up in my own stupidity that I almost stumbled over Cory, who was sitting on the porch waiting for me. I remembered I hadn't seen him at the game, which was unusual.

"Cory?"

He didn't answer.

"Cory, is something wrong?"

"I'm in trouble."

He turned his back to me, walked to his car, and slumped against the fender.

"You don't need to tell me, Cory."

He squatted on the curb, his head bent over.

"Cory, I think I know what's wrong. I want to understand how you feel, but I don't know if I do."

He wrapped his arms around his stomach and began rocking back and forth. "Your mother said you had gone to the game, but I waited for you. I had to talk to someone."

"Do you want to come inside?"

"No, I just want to sit here. I don't want your mother to know."

I sat down on the curb next to him.

"I didn't want it this way. I just wanted some fun and to be with the frat guys. I even quit after talking to you. You talked to me too late, Seth. I'd already met Terry, and now she says she's—"

He started crying. I looked at him, but he turned his head away from me.

"It hurts. Why does God make it hurt so bad?"

"Maybe He doesn't cause the hurt. Maybe we do it to ourselves, and He only allows it. My grandpa says it's so we won't forget we're his sons."

I looked at him again. He was having trouble breathing. "Cory? Are you all right?"

"You were always close to God. Ask Him to stop the hurting."

I placed my arm across his back and tried to comfort him. I don't remember all we said. I remember the gentle rocking of his body, his swollen eyes. Somewhere I forgot my guilt and his rocking stopped. When we finished talking, he turned to me to say thank you. I recognized a certain familiarity in his face. He was beginning to control the hurt, shutting it inside.

"I'm all right now. I'm sorry. Look at me crying like a little kid."

"Have you told anyone else?"

"No, just you. I'll have to talk to my parents. It's going to kill my dad. At least I don't have to face him for a while. He's away on business."

"Cory, are you sure?"

"She went to the doctor today."

"What are you going to do?"

"I've been thinking about that while I waited for you. Terry said she thought her dad would send her out of state to have the baby, but I don't think I could live with myself knowing she was going through that while I stayed here."

He paused for a few moments. He'd need courage to live up to the decision he was making. "I'm going to marry her."

Wiser people would have thought of hundreds of things to say to Cory. He would need to worry about so many things now. But only one question was in my mind. "Cory? Do you love her?"

There was no wall, just a slight questioning fear. "I don't know, Seth. I don't even know what it means now."

17

Graduation

Cory was married that summer in the bishop's house. He finished the school year and went to work on a construction crew. His parents set him up in a little basement apartment a few blocks from the high school. When I started my senior year, Cory became a father.

I walked past the apartment every day after school and stopped by a number of times. Cory was there only part of the time. The marriage seemed to be working—at least they appeared happy. As Cory got busier, though, he was there less often, and I found it difficult to talk just to Terry. They never came to church. After a while we just drifted away from each other. I didn't see much of him the rest of my senior year.

Maybe that's what started it. Our senior year was supposed to be the final step into adulthood, when one leaves home with one's friends, going together into the world. But my friends were separating. My sisters both went to Brigham Young University that year. Mom and I seemed to rattle around the house. Viet Nam was becoming a personal reality. Laughter and innocence seemed to be slipping away.

During the first weeks of school I found out that I had enough credits to graduate if I went only a half day. I dropped four of my classes and worked at the air base in the afternoon. I began to hate school more and more. The only class I enjoyed was world literature. I spent hours in my room reading Steinbeck, Wolfe, and Camus.

The second week of school Shawn and four other frat friends were expelled for drinking. His dad had him back in the next day. We saw less and less of each other. I stuck with Larry, even though he still teased me. The biting edge was gone now. Andy was as fun as ever. Life didn't seem to matter to him—all he wanted to do was play his guitar. I tried to talk him into rooming with me at the 'Y', but he didn't have the grades to get in, so I tried to get him to study.

"Andy, if you don't get your grades up, you'll end up in Viet Nam."

"I know. The draft's getting bad, isn't it?"

"Then get your grades up."

"Why didn't we worry about Viet Nam until this year? I always thought our senior year would be the most fun, not the one with the most problems."

"If you'd stop playing your guitar and start studying, you could do well on the ACT. Those scores count a lot."

"It's too late now. Besides, I'm not going to take the ACT."

"Andy, you don't want to go to Viet Nam. My uncle turned into an alcoholic because of a war."

I read constantly and studied hours for the Teacher's Association Scholarship, working and reworking my essay. It never satisfied Miss Woodall.

"You're writing is changing, Seth. Stop reading all the modern authors. You've lost your wonder and delight of life. I can feel it in the words you use. Read the romantic English poets for a change. All of life is not lived in a minor key."

"Mine seems to be going that way lately. I need this scholarship so I can get out of this state."

"You told me once you had a big savings account."

"I want to use that for a mission for my church."

"Why don't you go to USC? It'll save you thousands of dollars in living expenses."

"Too close to home. I've got to go to BYU."

"Then lighten the tone of your writing. These are positive people who judge the essay. And, Seth, have a little confidence in your writing. You're young and inexperienced, but you've read old books."

But everything was falling apart. Just before graduation the final blow struck. Somebody had been arrested using drugs at the junior high school. At first I paid no attention—everybody talked about drugs, but nobody used them. It sounded like the stories that were always circulating about spiders in ratted hair. One day Larry talked to me about it.

"I've heard rumors," I told him, "but I don't believe them."

"Don't you know who it is?"

"I'm not at school much since I took the job at the air base. Who's going to do drugs with the junior-high students, anyway?"

"Mark. Wasn't he an old friend of yours?"

"Larry, it can't be true! Drugs are in San Francisco, not in high school!"

"I'm sorry, Seth. I thought you knew."

For the first time in my life, I ditched classes and work and spent the afternoon walking. Everywhere I walked I could see Mark, then Cory, Shawn, and Andy. They were laughing, talking, running late to classes, on the steps, crossing the streets, driving in every car that passed. They haunted the city with memories, misting in and out of the faces I saw. I returned to the school and faced the buildings.

"What have you done to us? You breed the bullies and the beer parties. You've destroyed their lives. None of us started out badly. We were all good until we came to you."

They gave Mark a choice. If he enlisted, they'd wipe his record clean and wouldn't pass charges. He chose Saigon. So I read, burying myself in another world. College couldn't come fast enough. I received a four-year scholarship to BYU, and a month before graduation my essay won the Teacher's Association Scholarship. My escape from California was secure. Somehow, life in Provo would be better.

During those last months of confused emotions, I had a physical examination. Our family doctor sat me down in the office and explained the results.

"For the last five years I've wondered why you were so small. Your family on both sides are tall, aren't they? And your sisters are both tall?"

"Yes."

"Seth, there's a chemical hormonal imbalance in your body. I should have noticed it before, but I wasn't really looking. However, it's easily corrected."

"It's not serious?"

"No. I can give you a series of shots over the next six months. They will straighten out the imbalance, and you should grow a good six inches, maybe more."

It worked. I grew eight inches and was over six feet tall when I graduated. I watched my clothes shrink away and wondered. So much could have been different. What began as a question turned into frustration.

All these years I've struggled, wondering why I was so small, wondering if I would ever grow, if I would ever be a man. And the answer was so simple. The doctor could have found it in a dozen other examinations. Why was it hidden, why was it allowed? For two years I couldn't even smile. Couldn't You trust me if You gave me what everyone else had? Didn't You think I would come to You without those fears and inferiorities?

I didn't want the answers. Those memories were painful, and I didn't want to relive them. It was over. I wanted it all behind me.

June and graduation came, a hot 110-degree southern California day. The auditorium was sweltering, yet we had to wear caps and gowns. All the parents pushed the capacity of the auditorium to its limits. There were more than eight hundred in my graduating class. I stared into the parents' faces as their sons and daughters were called.

"Melanie J. Bradford."

"George M. Bradley."

The names who weren't called haunted me.

Mark was in the jungles of southeast Asia.

"Joseph L. Brown."

Cory was working the night shift, living in a two-room apartment.

"Victor F. Bruce."

Shawn was moving into the mountains with some of his friends, like a hippie.

"Donald C. Burton. Kathy Burton." The names rolled on and on.

I looked for Andy and smiled at him. He was dreading this night. I had talked to him while we were putting on our caps and gowns.

"When do you report, Andy?"

"Two days after graduation. I'm barely going to make it."

"Then what?"

"Boot camp and overseas duty."

"Viet Nam?"

"By the end of the summer."

I turned back to the front and heard my name called.

"Seth Michaels, winner of this year's Teacher's Association Scholarship."

When commencement was over I stripped off my cap and gown and turned them in. I was third in line. I greeted my family, and we drove away from the school. I opened my diploma and saw that nothing was inside.

"My diploma isn't here."

"You pick it up Monday at the office," my sister said. "Didn't you hear the principal's announcement?"

"I guess not."

"They have to check the final grades and any fines."

It was the last slap in the face. I would have to go back again.

Monday morning I dragged myself down to the school to pick up the diploma. Seniors were everywhere, signing yearbooks and emptying lockers. The halls were littered so badly they looked like the city dump. I made my way through the crowds to the principal's office. I waited for over an hour, but finally got the diploma. Then I ran for the car.

As I hit the curb, I heard someone calling my name. Larry was running rapidly in my direction. I was itching to get in the car, but he was all out of breath when he reached me, so I had to wait a minute before he could talk.

"I'll probably never see you again, Seth," he started. "I know I haven't been the best of friends to you these past years. Look, I want to apologize for teasing you so much."

"Larry," I broke in, "don't worry about it."

"It's hard to say. I just wanted you to know that of all my friends, you're the only one I respect. I wish I were more like you." He looked me full in the face. "Anyway, I felt I wanted to tell you. Good luck at college. Maybe we'll see you around during vacation."

He turned and hurried down the sidewalk. I watched him run into the administration building, and suddenly the anger and bitterness were swept from my heart. I wanted to find Larry. I raced across the lawn and around the corner into the building, but he was gone.

The open, heavily littered hallway spread out before me. The hallway I had feared and hated, longed never to see again, echoed my name over and over. I walked up the steps as if I had been gone for years, and looked down the passageways of half-opened lockers full of discarded notebooks and covered with graffiti.

I had never been here before. The hallways and classrooms seemed entirely new, yet I had walked them for three years.

"You're the only one I respect." Every locker whispered his words. And I felt unworthy. I walked the entire campus, going into even the forbidden zones. A door slammed, and a group of girls, still clutching their yearbooks, ran down the corridor. A longing swelled and moved me down the halls.

How many times had He walked these same halls with me as a friend, I wondered. "Teach me, Father. I am willing to learn because a friend holds me in respect and only You understand."

You once asked for a miracle to keep you good. I gave you the last six years.

"And Mark? Cory? Andy? Shawn? What of them, Father. What of them?"

Life is not over in eighteen years, Seth.

I left the building and crossed the quad. When I got to the curb, I stopped one last time and looked at the administration building. A group of students climbed the stairs to get their diplomas. I held my own in my hand, fingering it reverently. Life was not over in eighteen years—theirs or mine.

PART 3

The Price of Truth

But we are all as an unclean thing,
And all our righteousnesses
Are as filthy rags;
And we all do fade
As a leaf;
And our iniquities,
Like the wind,
Have taken us away.

And there is none that calleth upon
Thy name,
That stirreth up himself
To take hold of thee:
For thou hast hid thy face
From us,
And hast consumed us,
Because of our iniquities.

But now, O Lord,
Thou art our father;
We are the clay,
And thou our potter;
And we all are the work
Of thy hand.

Be not wroth very sore,
O Lord,
Neither remember iniquity
For ever;
Behold,
See,
We beseech thee,
We are all thy people.

Isaiah 64:6-9

18

War

War fever seemed to permeate everything that summer. It was always in the news. More boys were dying, America was becoming more and more deeply involved, and the protests to the draft were becoming more and more frequent. Songs on the radio chanted anti-war slogans, and many of the kids my age were relating to them. I met men daily at the air base who had been to Viet Nam. They rarely spoke about it. I knew I wouldn't get drafted because of a school deferment, but I thought about Mark and Andy constantly. Though I hadn't talked to Mark in two years, I still considered him my friend.

Andy went to Viet Nam at the end of the summer. I called his father a few times, but the news was always the same—"Andy seems fine." I wondered why he was so calm about everything, but then I didn't really know him very well.

At the end of August I quit work and began packing for school. The day before I left, Mark's mother called.

"He's home from Viet Nam," my mother told me. "She thought you might like to know."

"He's been discharged?"

"He stepped on a land mine and lost his leg from the hip down."

All my war fears doubled.

"Maybe you should go see him. I think that's why his mother called."

"I haven't talked to him in years."

"He used to be your closest friend—maybe you owe him a visit."

"I know, but what do I say about his leg?"

"If you faced the war, Seth, you might not worry about Andy so much."

"Maybe I'd worry about him more."

I drove over to the house later that afternoon and knocked on the door. His mother was surprised to see me in spite of the phone call. She led me through the cluttered house, which hadn't changed much over the years, into the den, where Mark was watching television.

"Don't take too long, Seth. He's still not really well and sometimes gets overexcited."

Mark didn't recognize me at first, then he smiled and asked me to sit down. I sat across from him, my eyes riveted to his face.

"Go ahead. Look at it if you want to. Until you do, you won't feel at ease."

He hunched over to one side and raised the tiny bit of stump that still remained. I had to look at it. It didn't bother him at all, but I got pale and lightheaded.

"You going to BYU soon?"

"We're leaving for Provo tomorrow."

"I hear you got a big scholarship."

"I was lucky."

"Major?"

He seemed to look through me to the wall behind.

"I guess English. I never got over liking to read."

"You still have all that money in the bank from your dad?"

"It's still there. I'm using it for a mission."

The conversation lagged. I caught myself looking at the neatly creased fold of pantleg next to his hip. I jerked my head back to his face.

He was watching me.

"Horrible, isn't it?" His tone changed.

"I'm sorry, Mark. I didn't mean to stare."

"I stared the first time too. All day long I stared. At first I didn't know I had lost it. I was on a patrol one minute, and the next thing I knew I was in a hospital. I guess I was lucky—I never felt any pain. That was my first thought when I came to. I didn't hurt anywhere. Then I noticed my leg was numb—I couldn't move it."

He was talking rapidly now, and loudly. His mother came running into the room. Mark kept talking.

"I got scared because I couldn't feel my leg. I screamed, 'I can't feel my leg! I can't feel my leg!'"

His mother sat down next to him and put her arm around his shoulders. Mark didn't notice.

"The nurse didn't say anything to me. She just stared at me and started crying. Then I knew. I wanted to kill every Viet Cong in southeast Asia."

His mother shook him and said, "Mark, you don't need to worry anymore."

"I wanted to kill them all. But not now. Not now. I'm all done fighting. I don't want to fight again."

"Mark, I'm sorry about the war. I wish it could have been different for you."

"Don't wish that. I needed the war. I'm only sorry it didn't come sooner." He looked at his mother, then back at me. "If you're going to wish something for me, wish that I had what you have, what we both had when we were young. We were good friends then, weren't we? Now you're going to BYU, and I'm sitting here without a leg."

"I'm sorry I've upset you."

"Why did you come?"

I shook my head.

"You felt guilty, didn't you, Seth?"

He pinned me to the chair with his voice.

"You should have stayed with me, Seth. You were my one chance. I was turning bad, but we were friends. You started running with new friends, but they went wrong too, didn't they? I know about them. You going to leave them, too?"

His mother pulled him closer to her. "You can't say that, Mark. Seth, he's still not over the war. Don't mind what he's saying."

Mark stared at me. "It's true—he knows it's true."

I looked at his leg this time, not his face. "Maybe I could have helped more. I'm sorry. I was only thirteen, and I was afraid I might do some of the things you were doing. But our lives aren't over yet."

He looked at me for a long time, his eyes wide and confused. "No, my life isn't over. But eighteen years and my leg are gone. Can you tell me what's going to happen now?"

His mother nodded toward the door, trying to smile as she did so. I said good-bye to Mark, then his mother closed the door so he couldn't hear us.

"Don't feel badly about what he said. Most of what's happened is his own fault. He hasn't accepted that yet."

"There's always a battle, isn't there, Sister Allred."

"For Mark there's always been one. Maybe it's over now."

"What he said just now, it hurt."

"He would have destroyed you too, Seth, if you had gone with him."

"If I'd been stronger, maybe he would have gone with me. You know, I always secretly envied him being able to fight. I think he knew that."

"He still carries his own blame—don't try to carry it for him."

My grandparents visited us the last part of August. Grandpa asked to see my diploma as well as my scholarship certificates.

"I'm real proud of you, Seth. What did you do for this scholarship?"

"I had to write an essay on a major author."

"Who did you pick?"

"Matthew Arnold."

"'Ah, love, let us be true
To one another! for the world, which seems
To lie before us like a land of dreams,

So various, so beautiful, so new,
Hath really neither joy, nor love, nor light,
Nor certitude, nor peace, nor help for pain;
And we are here as on a darkling plain
Swept with confused alarms of struggle and flight,
Where ignorant armies clash by night.'"

"You memorized that passage?"

"When I was younger. I've loved it for years, although I never believed in its philosophy. The words are beautiful, though."

"It was the central poem of my essay. Miss Woodall made me refute it."

"Are you going to study literature in college?"

"Miss Woodall says I'm not good for anything else."

"What will you do with it when you graduate?"

"Probably teach."

"And write?"

"Maybe a little."

"I've always wanted to write—poetry mostly. I never got much of a chance. Jens wanted to write. He quit college to start a novel, but the war came, and when he got back, he didn't want to anymore. I tried to get him interested again, but he had other things on his mind. So you're going to try to write. That would be wonderful."

"I could never write like Arnold."

"Do you love words?"

"When they're arranged right."

"Then you could write that way. Do you mind if I quote one more passage?"

"No, go ahead."

"Words are God's chiseled stones, carved and rounded with spirit and symbol, through which I will one day build Temples of Meaning that will lift man's mind upward as surely as these granite walls lift his eyes."

"Who wrote that?"

"I did, when I was young. I was sitting on the lawn next to the Salt Lake Temple. But I built houses instead. Maybe my grandson could build those temples I always dreamed about."

"Why are you telling me all this, Grandpa?"

"Because I'm a meddlesome old man trying to plan my grandson's life."

"I don't mind. Would you write that sentence down for me, the one about Temples of Meaning?"

"I'll say it again and you write it."

The next day I escaped to college. There was no intolerance, no fighting, no drugs, wild parties, or Viet Nam at the 'Y.' The campus was beautiful, and everyone was friendly. Everywhere I turned, Mormons smiled and talked to one another. Girls strolled the campus in small groups with returned missionaries stalking after them.

I was hoping my roommate would be there when I arrived, but the room was empty. I loafed around, meeting other freshmen, until he arrived. He was a junior from Washington who looked like John Lennon without hair. His frame was long and jointed, held together by sleeves and pantlegs. I asked him if I could help him set up his things, but he declined my offer. He didn't seem to be very outgoing.

I ate at the cafeteria while he put his things away, then went back to the room. As soon as I opened the door, my dream of peace came to a bitter end. On the floor, carefully spread out to serve as our rug, was a huge American flag. I just stood in the doorway and stared. My roommate pushed by me, walked across the flag, and lay down on his bed.

"You might as well get used to me now," he said. "We're going to spend a year together."

He glared at me. I went to the head resident and asked for a room transfer.

"Why?" I was asked.

"He's a Viet Nam protester!"

"Aren't you overstating the problem a bit?"

"We'll argue."

"I can't change you just for that reason."

"I have a friend in Viet Nam."

"Try to get along, Seth."

With the memory of Mark on my mind, I stormed back to the room and swept the flag from the floor. A corner of it caught on the bed frame and it ripped a hole across the stars. I handed it to him.

"This means nothing to me," he said. "I don't respect it."

"I do."

"That flag cost me ten dollars. You tore it, you buy it."

"Twenty-five thousand students, and I get a Viet Nam protester."

"Even paradise has a few realists."

He crumpled the flag into a little ball and stuffed it into the bottom of his drawer.

"Ten bucks," he said.

"When I can."

I spent two weeks trying "not to run away from my problems." He always wanted to talk about the war, and he kept on hounding me about the ten dollars.

"I need that money," he said.

"I'll bet your wallet screams when you take it out of your pocket."

"Ten dollars, and I want it in cold, hard cash."

"Tomorrow."

I bought all the ice cube trays I could find, and a box of garbage bags. Then I went to the bank and got twenty rolls of pennies. I carried them to Becky's apartment.

We froze pennies for ten hours. I slept on the couch. An alarm clock woke me up every two hours. By seven in the morning I had my thousand cubes, the first batch getting smaller by the minute. Becky drove me to the dorm. I struggled up to the third floor with five garbage bags of ice cubes, pushed open the door, and dumped them on the floor.

"Here's your ten dollars. Just like you wanted it—cold, hard cash." I opened the drawer, scooped some ice cubes into it, and took out the flag. "It's mine now. I just bought it."

I didn't wait to see his reaction, just turned and walked to Jan's.

"What did he say?"

"I didn't give him the chance. I just walked out."

"Oh, Seth. You'll be in trouble with the dorm."

"I'm not sorry. I felt I owed it to Mark and Andy."

"You keep blaming yourself for their being in Viet Nam."

"I got a letter a couple of days ago from Andy. At the end of it, he said, 'I shot at the Viet Cong for the first time. I don't know if I hit anyone. I hope I never know.'"

"The war isn't your fault, Seth. Did it make you feel any better to dump ice cubes all over the dorm floor?"

"It doesn't make me feel any better about Andy, but here I am going to football games and eating doughnuts at the Wilkinson Center while Andy—I just had to do something. Haven't you ever felt that way?"

"You want to stay here tonight and put off going back? But just for one night."

The next evening I returned to the dorm. My roommate had threatened to sleep in the hall. The head resident arranged a room change. After the change my life brightened considerably.

19

Familiar Fears

My new roommate was a lot like Andy, except that he spent every spare minute pining over his girlfriend back home. I caught him one morning trying to spoon out her initials from his alphabet cereal.

"You like her that much?"

"It's bad, isn't it?"

"Do you do the same thing with soup?"

"Haven't you ever loved anybody?"

"Not that way."

"Never? I can't believe that."

"I guess I'm just one of the enigmas of the universe."

"You never did anything crazy over a girl?"

"Once maybe."

"What did you do?"

"I carried an arrowhead in my wallet during junior high school."

I hadn't thought much about Jaimie for the last few years. I had taken the arrowhead out of my wallet in high school, but a nagging thought had been running through my mind. Now I finally gave in to it.

"Hand me the student directory, please. I want to look up a name," I said.

I ran down the Nortons. Midway through the page I found her name. "She's here," I muttered, but he heard me.

"Who?"

"The girl who gave me the arrowhead. Here's her name."

"You sure it's the same girl?"

"No, but she was a Mormon and would be a freshman this year. Besides, there's only one Jaimie Norton."

"Call her."

"That was years ago. She wouldn't even remember me. She'd think I was nuts."

"You haven't been at BYU very long, have you?"

Two days later I walked over to her dorm. When I knocked, a blond girl opened the door and smiled.

"Hi!"

"Does Jaimie Norton live here?"

The smile became serious. "Yes."

"Does she have reddish brown hair and light green eyes?"

"Kind of like that. Do you want to come in?"

"No, I'll wait here."

"Do you want me to get her for you?"

"Is she from Oregon?"

"Pendleton."

"Ask her if she ever found a white Indian awl."

"An Indian awl?"

"It's an arrowhead, long and pointed with a scallop on top."

"I'll ask her. Maybe you'd better wait out here." She smiled again and disappeared into the dorm. I had about decided that I had the wrong Jaimie when the blond girl returned.

"Is your name Seth?"

"Yes."

"Do you have an uncle named Morgan who catches mice?"

"It's her!"

"Can you come back in a few hours?"

"Why?"

She gave me a look of exasperation. "She can't see you right now."

"This afternoon after class?"

"I think that will be fine."

I returned four hours later. Jaimie answered the door. She hadn't changed much. She was a few inches taller, and her hair was longer, but her eyes could still read my thoughts, and she had the same high, clear voice that showed every emotion.

"Seth?"

"A taller version."

"You're a freshman?"

"For the last few weeks."

"Do you want to come in for a while?"

"Your roommate thinks I'm strange. How about the Wilkinson Center instead?"

Within an hour I knew more about Jaimie than any other girl next to my sisters. She was majoring in music. She wanted to go to Wales and hear an all-male choir sing in an old Celtic castle and then tour the rest of Britain. She had five brothers, two of them older than Jaimie, and a three-year-old baby sister. She skied with her family, made homemade bread her father called pharaoh's bricks, and watched football with her brothers. When I took her to the BYU games she explained the referee calls to me and told me why the plays didn't work. She liked the ocean better than the mountains. I asked her why.

"It's more musical and has orange sunsets, and it affects your moods more."

She liked dresses with high collars—"If I don't have to make them." She loved to read almost as much as I did and had one weakness—an insatiable appetite for M & M's.

"I have an attack every few days."

She had a core of stability that I grew to believe nothing could ever trouble. In the next three weeks I took her out five times. The fifth night out "The Frog" died. My roommate found out about it and had a special cake made. On the top was a picture of a frog floating feet-up in the water and the words, "It couldn't have happened to a nicer guy."

Within a few weeks she could read me better than Andy could. The week of general conference she asked when I had last seen my father.

"He was down the first week of school. He took my sisters and me to dinner."

"He never remarried in all these years?" she asked.

"He lives alone in Salt Lake. I think he has a cat."

"He must be lonely."

"I thought so when I was little, but I wonder now. Maybe he likes it that way."

"You should go see him and spend a weekend there."

"Why?"

"Do you need a reason? He's your father."

"It's not the same. In the past years I've seen him maybe five times."

"You get all tense when you talk about him. How come?"

"I guess I don't know how to feel about him. He's always been a mystery. Something there, but not there."

"That's why you need to go see him."

"Jaimie, would you mind if we didn't talk about him?"

"I'm sorry."

I didn't want to see him, but Jaimie's eyes held a tiny hurt look that tried to understand. I finally called him. "Dad. This is Seth." I didn't get an answer so I went on. "General conference is this weekend. I've never been able to go. If I can get a ride up, could I stay with you over the weekend?"

"Don't get a ride. I'll come and get you."

Thursday night I drove back to Salt Lake City with him. For the first time in my life I walked into his home. It was beautiful. Every room was decorated professionally and filled with copies of great art works. On the piano was a marble copy of Michelangelo's *Pieta*.

He led me to the den. Three walls were lined from floor to ceiling with books. There were no paperbacks. I drew my breath.

"I'd give anything to have a room like this."

"It's yours for the weekend. The couch under this painting pulls out into a bed. Go ahead and look over the books."

Every major author was there. In the center was a set of leather-bound classics that covered four shelves.

"You're majoring in literature, aren't you? Your mother told me your essay won a scholarship."

"Have you read all of these?" I asked.

"Most of them."

"These leather ones?"

"Several times."

"Grandpa would have loved this room."

"I'm an English teacher."

I pulled a classic from the shelf. The leather slid through my fingers, soft, like spring moss. I smelled the leather and the strong, full odor of ink locked between the pages.

"I never knew you had a room like this."

"Not many people do. Sit and read. I'll go fix you some dinner. I've learned to be a fairly good cook over the years. And don't mind Pharisee there—he thinks this is his room."

A large white Persian cat was enthroned in regal comfort at the top of the sofa.

"What did you say his name was?"

"Pharisee. I thought he deserved a biblical name, and that one fits him. When he closes his eyes and purrs, you can almost hear him pray in grateful condescension that he was born a cat and not a human."

We ate dinner, drove to a sports mall for a swim and a sauna, then went back home to spend the rest of the evening. I spent Friday morning and afternoon at conference. At the close of the afternoon session, Dad was waiting for me at the north gate of Temple Square.

A wall of protection and apprehension still existed. I sat on the couch that night and watched him when he wasn't aware. The wall troubled me, yet in the den it faded.

I lay awake that night remembering the unshared hurt I'd seen in his face, and wondering what choices he had lived with over the years.

The questions came flooding back in the darkness of the room. I turned on the light. I looked for clues in what I remembered about our conversations, in the passages he'd underlined in his books, in the marble statues and brushed oil copies of Europe's greatest artwork. I found no answers, just an existence, a life. I turned the light off, and the room disappeared into blackness. I awoke remembering a hushed warning from my mother.

"Mother, will God tell you anything you want Him to?"

"If it's important enough to you. Remember though, before you ask Him, make sure you really want to know the answer."

I wasn't sure I wanted to know.

Dad drove me back to Provo Sunday night. The next morning Jaimie was waiting for me in the library. "How was your visit?"

"A little uncomfortable sometimes."

"But not bad? Did he go to conference with you?"

"I asked, but he said people in Salt Lake weren't supposed to go. I think he felt he didn't fit in."

"Tell me about the whole visit."

"He has a room full of books, all the classics bound in leather. He bought them in England. We read most of the weekend. It wasn't bad in the den, almost natural, but he didn't say anything very important."

"Are you going back?"

"Next weekend. You don't mind? There's a game."

"No, I've got a paper due anyway."

I went back every other weekend for the next two months. Jaimie was always waiting, trying to help me work out my confusion. By the first of December I began to wonder why.

She wanted to see the lights on Temple Square. I borrowed Becky's car, but it snowed that day and was still snowing when evening found me at her dorm.

"Do you really want to go all the way to Salt Lake?" I asked her.

"Sure. Why not? You've already got your sister's car."

"I can get it another night."

"What's the matter with tonight?"

"No particular reason."

"It's the snow, isn't it?"

"Not really," I said.

"Yes, it is. Remember the first day it snowed? You hung on to me all the way across campus."

"It wasn't that bad."

"You were late for your next class, weren't you?"

"Class schedules are always arranged so your next class is across campus. Being late is part of the law here."

"You California guys are all the same. You forget you have knees when the walks are slippery."

"Well, I've never walked on ice before."

"Nor driven?"

"That's right. So now you know. Can we go another night?"

"I'll drive, or will that deflate your manly ego?"

"It would."

"You're just like my brothers. Give me the keys. You're going to your dad's next weekend, and this is my last chance."

"All right, but I'm not sitting next to you."

"Your loss. You can sit with your pride."

She opened the door for me and climbed in. We drove through the snow flurries to Temple Square and parked the car. In a few minutes we were walking under the universe of tiny stars that clung to every tree. The snow diffused the light, softened every feature, and placed us both into a reflective mood. We rested in one of the entrances to the tabernacle and looked through the flakes to the silver granite walls of the temple.

"Have you ever been here with your father, Seth?" She looked up at the temple, then back into my face.

"No, but Mother brought us here every summer."

"You should bring your Dad. It's a special place." She moved forward into the snow. I counted the snowflakes in her hair until there were too many. She didn't move.

"Jaimie, why did you give me the white awl?"

"That was years ago. Why do you want to know now?"

"I kept it in my wallet for a long time."

"You didn't."

"Why did you give it to me?"

"You wanted it. I told you I could always read your face."

"That's not the only reason."

"No. I knew you were hurting. I guessed it had something to do with your uncle."

"You were thirteen then. How could you have figured it out?"

"My dad says it's a gift."

"What kind of gift?"

"To feel what others are feeling."

"That's why you keep telling me to see my father, isn't it?"

The pinpoints of Christmas lights, thin and sharp, glistened through the crystals as they drifted down. She stepped back into the doorway.

"You're all knotted up over your father. I think you always have been, even when you didn't know you were. You want to know that he loves you. That affects all your relationships, and it always will until it's resolved."

"It's never been that important to me. Just sometimes things would happen, and I'd remember and wonder or get angry."

"It's been more important than you realize. You want him to say it and make you feel it. You want him to explain his life to you. Maybe he can't. Are you going to punish everybody around you for the rest of your life?"

"Would I believe him if he told me?"

"It wouldn't make any difference."

"It would have to make a difference, Jaimie."

"I have a great uncle. I was scared of him when I was little. He lived all alone, never married, never visited anyone, didn't have any friends. I wouldn't have known he even existed except that my father visited him every month. I went with Dad sometimes. My uncle had two fruit trees in the backyard. He planted them there so he could see them from his bedroom, and in the spring the blossoms filled the little house he lived in. He trimmed them and fertilized them every year. In the fall he bottled the fruit all by himself. He gave the trees names and referred to them as 'my children.'

"I asked my dad one day if he thought Uncle George was happy living there all alone. 'I think so,' he said. 'But he hasn't got anyone who loves him or takes care of him.' 'Is that what makes people happy?' he asked. I told him that's what made me happy. 'He's happy, Jaimie. He's got something to love, even if it's something that can't love him back.'

"The day he got so old he couldn't care for himself, we drove him to a rest home. He stood at the back window looking at his trees and cried. Then he said, 'Good-bye, trees.' There was love in his voice, and I knew that my dad was right.

"Everybody wants to be loved, Seth, but they need to *love* more than they need to *be* loved. Happiness comes from the loving. If you spend enough time with your father, maybe you'll learn to do that. It won't matter if he tells you he loves you or not."

I remembered the man who carried me on his shoulders by the ferris wheel and the happiness I felt loving him. "I had it once—maybe that's why I've never forgotten that first memory."

"What memory, Seth?"

"I've never told anyone." She tipped her head, and her hair fell down in front of her face.

"Jaimie, how can you know so much about love and life and be only eighteen?"

"Anybody can *learn* it. I haven't met the person yet who could *live* all of it. We're all a little bit too selfish."

"Not you."

"Yes, me. Why do you think I'm telling you these things?"

She left the cover of the doorway, walking into the snow and light. I followed her, but we talked of other things.

20

A Path for Every Runner

I missed spending the last weekend before Christmas with my father. I promised my roommate I'd help him with an English term paper. The project took us into the weekend. The semester ended a few days later. I said good-bye to Jaimie, gave her a tiny silver mouse on a chain for Christmas, and phoned my dad, thanking him for all the weekends. He said he looked forward to more weekends in the spring. Twelve hours later I was home with Mother, the smell of Danish pastry in the kitchen mingling with the pine of the Christmas tree, the packages, the stockings, the old Bing Crosby record, and the memories—all of them.

After Christmas I went to see how Mark was doing, but he had moved to his own apartment down the coast. Cory called to tell me they had another baby. I spent the afternoon with them. They were still living in the little apartment next to the school. Cory hadn't been back to church yet, but I noticed a well-used Book of Mormon on the lamp table and some missionary tracts. Cory told me that Andy would be home before the first of the year. He'd been wounded too.

I knew Andy would come and see me the moment he got home, so I waited. When he called, I invited him over. He had caught a piece of shrapnel in his back and was home for good on a medical discharge. A small piece had also struck his right cheek, tearing the muscle and distorting his mouth. The change was slight, but it was difficult for him to smile. We talked until everyone else went to bed, then our conversation turned to the war.

"It's so good to know you're alive and not maimed or crippled," I said.

"Like Mark?"

"I guess that's what I mean. Say, we don't need to talk about it."

"Why not? I don't mind. Let me tell you what I learned over there. There are only three things that matter."

He counted them off his fingers one by one. "Friendship, freedom, and truth. Until I got to Nam I didn't know what any of them meant.

"We never knew that friendship, Seth. When you sit back to back with your buddy in the heat and mud, your life is in his hands, and his is in yours. He's your real friend, and the only one that matters. Sometimes you don't even know his name. You and I—we were just boys."

He held up his second finger.

"Freedom! We don't know what it means to be free in America.

"We took turns being point man on our patrols," he continued. "It was my turn. No one liked to be there because he was always the guy that got whatever came first. We were patroling a dense area of jungle, so dense you couldn't see fifteen yards ahead of you. I came around a corner and there, not ten yards away, was a Viet Cong patrol. Their point man was a boy who couldn't have been much older than fourteen. I could see his eyes! They were full of fear. He was inexperienced. His rifle was pointed off to the side instead of straight ahead like it should have been.

"For a few seconds we both just stood there and stared at each other. Then I could see his gun moving ever so slowly in front of him.

"I didn't want to shoot him. I tried to think of him as my enemy, but he was only fourteen. If he'd been out in the jungle and I hadn't seen his eyes, it would have been easier, but I could see the fear.

"I learned then what freedom is. You're free only when no man can make you do what you don't want to do, don't believe is right to do. I had to shoot a boy—a boy, Seth!—because I was an American and he was Viet Cong. I hated the men that made me pull that trigger. But I had to pull it. Seth, I waited until the last second, but he was going to shoot me. I prayed, 'God, don't make me kill this boy!' I said it right out loud, but I had to. I pulled the trigger and saw his face the second he knew he was going to die. That's when I learned what truth was. Truth is just staying alive. Not religion, not ideals, just making sure it was him that got the bullet and not me. Seth, when we were kids—"

He made it sound as if it were a long time before, but it had been less than a year.

"—you used to tell me all the things God did for you, and I believed you. I could never make it work for me, but I thought it was because you seemed to really need God and I never did. Then the one time in my life I really wanted Him and really needed Him, He didn't answer. Maybe He didn't have time to answer—He was too busy somewhere else. I don't say He isn't there, but if He is there, He doesn't care. At least He doesn't care about me and half a million people in Viet Nam. God may have blessed America, but He cursed the rest of the world. So I thought if God doesn't care about Viet Nam, then I don't either. What I do here is not my fault. After that it was easy to kill. I even got to enjoy it."

"What seems to be isn't always the truth, Andy. God does care."

"Not about me!"

"About everyone. Don't let the war blind you. He does love us."

"Love? Love, Seth? You weren't there. You didn't crawl like a reptile through the swamps. Darwin was right, we did come from the slime and muck. He made only one mistake. After we had evolved to the noble state of man, we crawled back into the mud again, and we've been there ever since. Whatever progress we've made is only a backwash of our own greed and lust."

"You don't believe that, Andy. They're just words. I've read them a hundred times from greater minds than ours."

"I don't believe anything. Don't you see? Viet Nam snuffed out that flame. There's nothing left."

"Don't you want to light it again, Andy, now that you're home?"

"I can't forget what I've seen, what I've experienced."

"You can't stay this way. Not you."

"Still trying to look out for me, aren't you? Well, Seth, I've grown up. I'm a man now. I'm not going to struggle to believe in God like you do anymore. I tried. He wouldn't help me."

"Andy, for the first time in my life, you make me doubt. Not God's existence, but His love."

"Don't you dare stop believing, Seth. I'm not going to carry that burden. I always wanted to believe like you."

"Andy, you don't understand. It's more than just you. It's everyone. The only difference between you and me is God."

"There's no condemnation for me or reward for you. I've learned that truth, Seth. But you go on believing. He is God to you."

"How do you believe in that kind of God, Andy?"

I walked to the door with him and watched him disappear down the road. Then I went to my bedroom and knelt.

"Father, I doubt. I can't ignore it as much as I want to. I've tried to ignore my fears when their lives were falling apart. I never asked the questions. I'm asking them now. You have to understand how it looks to me. Life's been unfair for all of my friends, and the war is the greatest injustice of all. They never asked for it. It was unfair for Uncle Jens and Lars and my mother. Grandpa's feeling of failure is needless. You have blessed me continually in spite of my fears and disappointments, and that is the crowning proof of life's unfairness. I never faced what they faced. I doubt you. I can't believe as much as I used to. Maybe I never had any real faith. And if you answer this, Father, won't it prove Andy's right? Why should you come for me and not for Andy or the others?"

He said nothing, but an image began focusing in my mind, and I saw a thick forest of trees. Facing the trees was a trench. I was in the trench with Andy and Mark. A battle was about to begin. The trees formed a wall that rose higher and darker and seemed to move toward us. No forest was ever thicker, more alien, than that inscrutable mass of trees. My heart seemed to explode in apprehension at the growth of those black trees, and I knew that I would have to enter them. We would all have to enter them. I watched as legions of gaunt shapes, more mysterious because we sensed them without seeing them, took their positions behind the massive wall of the forest.

Far in the distance, behind the wall of trees, a light was shining. Through its intensity, the wall separated to show numerous paths running through the massed solidarity of the trees. One path lay directly in front of me.

The battle started. I ran. Someone fell on my left, then one in front of me. Ahead the black mass of forest rose higher than I ever imagined. It bore down on me, its blackness waiting to receive me. I saw another fall, and I faltered.

Don't look at the forest, Seth. Look at the path.

I entered the forest, felt it close around me like water. Hands gripped my ankles and arms, trying to pull me down. Thousands of hands grasped until their combined weight made progress through the trees almost impossible.

I pushed and twisted and tore at the hands until they grew fewer and finally disappeared. When I could feel them no longer, I stopped. I turned around to look behind me. There by the trench and in the first fringes of the forest lay my companions.

Do you understand?

"I understand that many die. I don't understand why you help some and not others?"

Is that your only question?

"I'm afraid to ask the other question."

What is in your heart, Seth?

"How can they help feeling the way they do? For some there is no way through the forest. What of them?"

Is that what lies deepest in your heart?

I reached through the past to the image I treasured as the brightest moment of my life, the feel of my father's cheeks and the spinning ferris wheel lights.

"Father. It's my father. I want to stop the hurt he's caused me, to make it not matter anymore. I want to love him and forgive him. Will you help me? But to do this I have to believe it wasn't his fault, that there was no way through the trees for him. He had to fall. Isn't that why they all had to fall?"

I cannot tell you their lives, but you must accept the truth. All love must be tempered with truth. There is a path for every runner, but some men choose the trees.

"It's awfully late, Seth."

"Yes, Mother, but I can't sleep."

"Do you want to talk?"

"Yes."

"Is it Andy?"

"He doesn't believe in anything now, not God, not people, not friendship. He made me feel like a little kid for still believing and that when I grow up I'll shed my beliefs like I did dragons and witches."

She sat down next to me and thought for a moment before answering. "Isn't it sad that some measure life by what they lose, when it should be measured by what they gain. Too many people throw away the strengths and beliefs of childhood and think they are mature for having discarded them. Andy had to look at a piece of life he wasn't ready to see."

"He says it made him see what life was really like, and now he knows the truth."

She looked over at me. "Andy knows less of life now than he did before he went to Viet Nam. To him life is ugly and cruel. I rebelled at the beautiful too because of the ugly and lost the lessons they both had to teach, but the beautiful is no less a part of life because it is beautiful. I finally realized that I was not running from life, but from my own inadequacies. It's not that the world is too base, too full of contradictions—we're too petty, too full of fear and pride."

"We all have those inadequacies," I said. "The ugliness and unfairness cause pain and hurt. Don't they make the price of happiness too great?"

"The purpose of living is to gain those things we need to answer the questions. When we run, we run from the one thing that can stop the running. Most people don't run from life because it's unfair. Life slips away from them because they are shallow. Life overflows. They run from the flood to keep from drowning, or sadder yet, pour out the happiness to make room for the misery. If our souls were deeper and stronger, we would know and love and understand as God does, but we shrink, we call life cruel, and blame God for our weaknesses. The fault lies with us—we don't want to face the struggle."

I looked down. "We all run in different ways, don't we?"

"And from different things."

"Uncle Jens?"

"Yes, and Lars too."

"Dad?"

"In his own way, and even me. Maybe I'm still running from that."

"Mother, I'm tired of all the conflicting feelings. I just want to give up."

"You're tired because you're still fighting. When you stop feeling tired, the fight will be over. When you begin to understand because you fought it through, there is always hope and joy. Eventually that's all a soul can hold. Anything less is less than life."

21

Through My Father's Eyes

During the rest of Christmas vacation, all my questions returned, then grew. The need to know became an obsession.

I went back to school feeling tired. I didn't return to see my father, because I wanted to understand before I saw him again. He called, inviting me up. I told him my new schedule was heavy, but I would try to get away. I spent the first two weeks dating Jaimie constantly, then reading till two or three in the morning. I began rereading the scriptures in preparation for my mission. Two days into Genesis I came to chapter 48, verses 5 and 10. Jacob was speaking to Joseph: "And now thy two sons, Ephraim and Manasseh, which were born unto thee in the land of Egypt . . . are mine; as Reuben and Simeon, they shall be mine. . . . And he brought them near unto him; and he kissed them, and embraced them."

It was the scriptural justification that would allow me to turn from my father to the love and security of the only man who had been a constant influence in my life, he who had lost his sons as I had lost my father.

I called Grandpa and asked him if I could come up and talk. I borrowed Becky's car and drove to Ogden. In a few hours I found myself on the couch in their room facing the old green rocking chair.

He came in and pulled the Bible from the drawer. It was still filled with notes and newspaper clippings. "What were you wondering about, Seth, that merited a trip all the way from Provo?"

"Grandpa, would you read Genesis 48, verse 5?"

I watched his garden-stained fingers flip through the pages of Genesis. A few scraps of paper fell to the carpet. I bent over and handed them to him while he found the verse. He handed the Bible to me. "Read it for me, will you please?"

I read it out loud, and he slowly raised his head, his powder-white hair pushed in every direction.

"Grandpa, I'm going on a mission in a few months. You've been closer to me and meant more to me than any other man I've known. And you've loved me like a son because I needed that. Even when we disagreed and I'd stop talking to you, I still loved you."

He ran his fingers lightly up and down the columns of his Bible.

"I know all about Uncle Jens, Grandpa. I know he drank himself to death. I know how badly it hurt you to lose him and then for Uncle Lars to leave the Church. I hurt too, Grandpa, because I always wanted a father. Even as a small boy I knew you cared about me more than my father did. I feel some things for him, Grandpa. I've shared some things with him this year, but I love you. May I be the Ephraim and Manasseh in your life to replace the Reuben and Simeon you lost? Would you let me be sealed to you in the temple?"

"I don't think it's possible, Seth. And you're sealed to your father."

"He won't be in the celestial kingdom like you will."

My grandfather closed the Bible with shaking hands. "What do you want with an old Dane? I'm almost ninety years old. The Lord has let me live a long time and see a lot of things. Do you know why, Seth?"

"Because you're good."

"No. He knew it would take that long to make a decent man of me. He could do it with other men in less time, but I was too stubborn."

He shifted the Bible to his knee and straightened it over the worn spot in his pants. "God gave me sons, and though I know I'm not to blame for everything, somehow I failed them. I learned how to grow great gardens, how to build beautiful houses, but not righteous sons."

He looked out the window. I followed his gaze to where the broken clods awaited another year's planting.

"You didn't fail me, Grandpa. You taught me to love the scriptures and about the voice inside."

"I wasn't a good father to my children. Perhaps I sowed the seeds for their failures. I can't cast that burden down, Seth. You're a man now. You must understand how a man feels."

"For me, Grandpa, you were everything a father could be. I don't care if you made mistakes. It doesn't matter to me. Please don't say no."

He laid his hand on my knee. "How can I say this to you, Seth, so you will understand and not be hurt? I have loved you all these years. I have taken pride in what you are accomplishing, in what you are becoming. Nothing will ever change that love. But Jens and Lars are my sons. They have done a lot of wrong things, maybe too many to ever be forgiven. Maybe they will never ask. But I hope, Seth. I hope that someday in the eternities something can be done. I can lose them only if I give up hope. Nothing would please me more than to be sealed to you as your father, but if we did this thing, we'd be killing the hope. It would be admitting that there was no redemption for them.

"It would be the same for you, Seth. Your father is no different than my sons. You must work with him and love him. Maybe he will seek forgiveness too. For their sakes, we must hold on, push aside our own desires, then leave the rest with God. Seth, we both carry the same burden. We can't lay it down—not yet, maybe not ever."

"What about my hope, Grandpa?"

He rose then, pulled me into his arms, and crushed me against the strength of his love. I smelled the warm flannel of his shirt. "Go to your father. Help him. You may be the only hope he has."

"But I don't love him as I love you, Grandpa. He'll never mean as much to me as you do."

"You go to him, Seth. Think how Reuben and Simeon felt to be replaced by their nephews even when they knew they had sinned. We must think of them. We must not be selfish."

"But he left me, Grandpa, of his own choice."

"Then you must forgive him, knowing that he left you."

I got back in the car and drove down the street. I knew Grandpa was right, but I couldn't love my father as long as the reason for his leaving remained a mystery. I had to know that part of his life, no matter what it meant in personal pain, no matter how ugly. Somewhere in his home was an answer.

"Oh, Father," I prayed, "let me find an answer.

I saw a phone booth, stopped, and dialed Dad's number. "Dad, can I stay over Monday? I need a quiet place to study. You'll be gone to work, and I can get it done."

"I'll come and get you."

"I'm already in Ogden. I have Becky's car. I'll be there in an hour."

He left for work at seven the next morning. I stayed in bed until he was gone, then waited a good forty-five minutes to make sure he would not return to the house.

I got up and began to search. I went room by room, but found nothing, just clothes, books, and art. I saw a linen closet at the end of the hall. I stopped in front of it and opened the doors. At the bottom of the closet were three drawers. I pulled the top drawer open. A set of pillow cases were carefully laid across the top. I removed them and saw an old shoe box filled with letters and papers, and next to it a photo album. The black binding was cracked and torn. I lifted it from the drawer.

I sat down in the hall and stared at the first page, neatly printed with "The Life of Paul S. Michaels" in his mother's hand. I thought of the hope in that simple announcement, then turned the page and saw the first picture of my father. It was centered in the middle of the page and bordered in white, with a lock of dark baby hair tied neatly to the corner. He was just a baby.

As I turned more pages, I watched him move through childhood, into early teens, and then into college. Amusement parks, picnics, school graduations, and vacations appeared, all neatly bordered in white. Every picture was carefully labeled with age, place, and circumstances. Then her handwriting stopped, and my father's handwriting began. The first picture was in front of the Salt Lake Temple the day he left for the mission field. Each succeeding picture was still labeled, now in more detail, but giving the same information—age, place, and circumstances. Companions, cities, and investigators spoke from the pages.

My mother came next, a full page covered with pictures of her, then my mother and father together. Jan and Becky appeared in the pictures on the next few pages. Each picture was neatly mounted to the page, meticulously labeled.

My own face as a newborn baby appeared, then my sisters and I together. The labels were missing now, only a date was scrawled across the border of the pictures. The pictures were not as neatly arranged, but were placed here and there across the pages—some weren't even mounted. Then, halfway through the album, the pictures stopped. I turned back to the last page of pictures and noticed the date—October 27, 1950—my first birthday, and the only one he had ever shared with me. He was holding me on one arm, his other hand proudly holding up one finger. I looked into the face in the picture. I remembered the feel of my hands on his cheeks and the whirl of the ferris wheel lights.

"He gave up the album, Father, gave it up, and relegated it to the bottom of the linen drawer because he had no memories to light the black pages. Perhaps his life has been emptier than mine, perhaps even more painful. But wasn't it his own fault? There is a path for every runner. Father, why?"

I lifted out the shoe box of old papers and letters. Everything was haphazard, but they were all important papers. I pulled out his high-school diploma, his missionary call, his first graduation certificate, a license to practice medicine, and finally his second college degree in English and a teaching certificate, but no answers.

I found an envelope stamped *Confidential* in red letters. I hesitated, then carefully opened it. It was a will, legally signed and notarized. I read the date—November 14, 1967. I skimmed through the legal talk at the beginning and came to the sentence that left all his books to me and all other belongings to be divided between my sisters and me. I resealed the envelope and placed it back in the box.

I reached for the next envelope. Underneath it on the bottom of the box, held together with a paper clip, were some ticket stubs. They were all from the same place. One of them was torn so I could still read the name printed in black letters—Lagoon. I clipped them together again and stared at them.

I could hear my father's voice pleading.

These are the only links with the children I walked away from. May I keep them, Seth? No one will ever know.

"You never came into the funhouse with us or rode the ferris wheel. We always went alone. I always wanted you to come with us, but you always said, 'Funhouses and rides are for children.'"

They were important to me.

"You never mentioned them, and I've been here weekend after weekend."

I can't, Seth. Do you understand? I can't.

"I can't understand. If you loved us, you'd have wanted to be with us and laugh with us."

I couldn't, Seth. Please understand. I never stopped loving you.

"But you left. A father can't leave and still love. I didn't understand it then—I can't now."

Will you let me keep them now that you know?

I took from the box an envelope marked *Beckworth and Sons* and another one from the Office of the First Presidency. My search ended here.

"What did he do, Mother?"

You must not ask me to tell you.

"But I have the answer in my hands. I have the envelopes."

We must remember only the good he has brought us. He brought you good, Seth. Even if you never experienced his love, he felt it.

"Let me open them, Mother."

You're risking everything to satisfy your curiosity.

"Don't I have every right to satisfy it? What about the missed father-and-son outings, the ordinations, Bert's missed confirmation."

He missed them, too. Forgive him. He fears those years, Seth, and what they cost you. Must you add your own wall to his?

"Mine? I've had to watch my friends building walls, but I've accepted them anyway. I remember Cory's confession."

Would you have forced that confession just to know?

"He wasn't my father. He didn't leave and hide the reasons."

I looked at the envelopes in my hand.

Will you open them, Seth, and take everything from him?

Then the other memories came, the reality of another Father who had guided me so freely through the years. So many times, in so many places, I had felt Him and known His love. Did those memories deserve the violation I wanted to commit? I sat on the floor holding the envelopes. Carefully I put them back in the box and slid the drawer shut.

22

In Another Man's Shadow

When the drawer closed, the unanswered question stopped its persistent nagging, and the joy and hope came as Mother had promised. God smiled in my heart and blew away the dried leaves of old pain so gently a baby's whisper would have seemed a hurricane by comparison.

I called Jaimie when I got back. We watched the students rushing from building to building. We slid across glazed patches of ice, rang the 'Y' bell with ice-packed snowballs, and made a giant snowman in front of Karl G. Maeser. She buried her mittened hand in the warmth of my pocket, clasping my hand. I dreamed of building empires once again.

"Do you know what I did today?" I asked her.

"Whatever it is, I hope it stays."

"Today I caught the roadrunner."

"You caught what?"

"I kicked Lucy's football and flew the kite over the tops of the trees."

"You're not making any sense at all."

"You never watched cartoons when you were little?"

"Sure. I never liked the coyote."

We walked downtown and tried to spend an imaginary $100,000. At seven I bought her dinner, then walked her back to the dorm. It was snowing again, a light Christmas snow. All the black, sand-streaked slush and melted footprints disappeared beneath the new white fold of wetness. It clung with powder lightness to every tree's stretching fingers, softening their scratching reach, wrapping every branch in whiteness.

"Can I ask you a question, Seth?"

"If it's not serious. I don't want to face any of life's paradoxes tonight."

She smiled and pushed together a little pile of snow with her feet. "It's an easy one."

"Okay, shoot."

"Remember that first summer at the ranch? What did you and your uncle do with that sack of mice?" She fingered the tiny silver mouse hanging from her neck.

"I'd be betraying an old family secret."

"I can hear your uncle telling you that. I can also hear him teasing when he said it." She carefully stepped into her little mountain of snow and made a perfect footprint.

"He was teaching me the law of the hunt."

"What hunt?"

"That's all I'll tell you, except one thing. The mice are never wrong."

She laughed, and her voice rippled through the snowflakes.

"Something happened this weekend," I said.

"I know. The knot's loosening."

"It's more than that."

"You talked to your father?"

"I know that he feels something, maybe even love. You'll tell me that's not as important as me loving him, but it's the first step—the rest may come later."

I walked home through the snow. It was almost eleven o'clock, and I was exhausted, but it was a weariness that felt good.

The next weekend I took Jaimie to Salt Lake City to meet my father.

He took us out to dinner and then to a play at the University of Utah. She was at ease with him almost from the first. I watched my dad. The tight lips were gone. I decided I would bring Jaimie with me the next time he asked me up for dinner.

Two weeks later I felt an uneasiness growing within me. I thought at first it was the winter. February snow has no softness or beauty. I had a lot of schoolwork, and so did Jaimie. There wasn't time for much else. We studied together in the library sometimes.

In the middle of March my cousin called from Logan. He was a freshman at the university. He was going out to the ranch to help move the cattle and wanted to know if I was interested. Early on a Friday morning we left for Nevada.

We moved cattle all day Saturday. It was cold with a wind that stung our eyes. The air was clear and spiced with the ever-present smell of sage. It was refreshing to ride again and watch Uncle Morgan bob and weave as he slowly fell asleep driving the cattle.

But the uneasiness didn't leave. So I spent as much time with Uncle Morgan as possible. Sunday night I sat with him, listening to him tell stories. Many I had already heard, but they had gotten better with age. I called his attention to it.

"A good story is always like that," he explained. "It grows, gathering new twists as it moves along with the man who's telling it."

He was delighted to hear I was getting along so well with Jaimie, especially when I told him what I gave her for Christmas.

"Why didn't you bring her with you?" he asked. "I'd have saddled you a couple of horses and let you wander down the canyon to the waterfalls."

"Is it a good place to race mice?" I asked him.

He laughed. It was a rich, deep sound, full of contentment. I thought of Mother's talk about having enough room in our souls and knew by the resonance of Uncle Morgan's laughter there was a cavern inside.

He flopped his hat on the kitchen table. "Do you remember the ward Christmas party your grandfather and I took you and your sisters to in Ogden?"

"You took me to a Christmas party?"

"You must have been about four. Your mother was trying to finish school. Your grandpa and I were assigned to take all the kids to the ward to see Santa Claus. After talking to Santa, you got it into your head that you were going to see his reindeer. He started to leave. You galloped across the floor and latched onto his leg. He couldn't get you off. Everyone was laughing, and you kept yelling, 'I'm going with you!'

"I think he wanted to hit you with his bag, but there were too many little kids watching. He leaned against the wall and tried to shake you off. You wouldn't shake. Finally your grandpa said to me, 'I guess we'd better go claim him—he's got our brand on him.'

"We couldn't get you off, Seth. Finally your sister Jan came over and talked to you. You let go, just like that, and Santa darted out the door."

"What did she say to me?"

"She told you that he wasn't the real Santa Claus, just the bishop or someone dressed up like him. The real one only came on Christmas. You shouted, 'If it was the real one, I wouldn't have let go!'"

On Monday we finished moving the cattle, and on Tuesday I returned to Provo. The uneasiness was still with me.

I woke about one in the morning. I'd had a dream, and I remembered every detail. I was running in an open desert. The sun made the sand's heat seep through the soles of my shoes. Giant trees stood all over the desert, growing out of the sand, but there were no shadows. I ran from tree to tree, circling each one again and again. The sun made a complete arc in the sky, but no shade formed around the trunks. Finally in the distance I saw a long tree on a rise. It towered above the other trees, casting a long refreshing shadow down the slope. I stepped into its shade and felt a coolness soothe my face. A voice came.

You have walked your whole life in another's shadow. Have you learned to be a man? Reach higher.

The shadow withdrew, pulling me with it until it came to the massive trunk, and then it disappeared. The trees slowly faded, and I was left alone in the sand and heat.

I was aware of an emptiness the moment I woke up. I had grown accustomed to His almost constant presence. Never had it occurred to me that it would be anything but permanent. The mountains were down, and all the earth was flat. I sat up, fearing that He would not return. The universe was between us. I cried across it.

"Father, why? You've always been there. I've never wanted you to leave."

I needed time to be alone. Jaimie noticed the change, but said nothing for two weeks. I wasn't the same with her. I stayed late in the library a few nights so I'd miss her calls. In the middle of the third week, she found me there. She closed my books gently without talking and waited by the table. I stood up and she slipped her arm into mine. We walked from the library to the lower campus.

"Don't be mad at me, Jaimie."

"I'm not mad. I'm hurt. What have I done? Don't I deserve an explanation?"

"I didn't know what to explain. It's not you."

"Is it your father?"

I stared at the pale green budding of spring on the trees. She sat on the grass and twirled a leaf between her fingers.

"You're all knotted up inside again, more than before."

"Yes, but in a different way."

"Why?"

"I'd rather you didn't know."

She bent her head slightly and hid behind the veil of her hair.

"Seth? Do—" She looked up at me. "How do you feel—"

"Please don't ask me that, Jaimie. Not now."

"Somebody's got to say something. You're going away this summer and then on a mission. I don't know what's inside you or how you feel about me. Something's happened, and you won't talk about it. I'm not going to go through two years wondering. You're meaning more and more to me, Seth Michaels, and if I have to kill those feelings, then I want to know now."

"I'm not sure what love is, Jaimie. I've been thinking about it the past few weeks. I saw it once that day in Nevada when my cousin got shot. I felt love in the arms of my grandfather and through the years from my mother. I have known love from many people, but I don't know if I've loved any of them back. You told me that, didn't you, Jaimie. I guess I wasn't listening."

I looked at her. She was crying.

"A few weeks ago I made one of the few unselfish decisions of my life. I crossed some kind of threshold because that mantle of nearness I've felt around my shoulders for all these years is gone now. Maybe I never really loved even Him. I suppose I did what He asked me to do so that He would love me more.

"You're right. I'm knotted up inside again, or maybe the knots were never really undone. I'm just learning how to untie them. He expects me to love everyone as He loves me, even my father. And it's hard. How can I love him if I can't forgive him for all those years?"

She looked at me with a touch as soft as dust on a butterfly wing.

"Let me help you, Seth. Don't shut me out. Don't run up the mountain again like you did on the ranch."

"Jaimie, this time I think I need to reach for love on my own."

We saw each other and talked through the end of the semester, but nothing came except the summer, and then we both went home.

In California I got a job driving a truck for the city. When I wasn't working I was studying. I tried to forget my father, but I found I couldn't. I memorized missionary scriptures, reread the standard works, and boned up on my French just in case I went to a French-speaking mission.

My call to Switzerland came in late September. I was to report to the Salt Lake Mission Home in the middle of October. I would turn nineteen while there. The bishop planned my farewell for the second Sunday in October.

The next few weeks were lost in a flurry of shopping, French study, and travel plans. The farewell was wonderful. All my old teachers and many of my friends and relatives came. They filled the chapel and halfway into the cultural hall. The four I really cared about didn't come, but I expected that. My Primary teachers couldn't believe I had made it this far. One of them told me she wouldn't have bet a nickel on my filling a mission if the Prophet himself had predicted it. I forgot for a while that I was going halfway around the world, that I wouldn't see my family for two years. But the meeting ended, and I went home alone with my mother and sisters to pack. I was going to Salt Lake City by train at eight o'clock.

I emptied my top drawer on the bed to go through nineteen years' worth of junk. The white Indian awl fell with the rest of the items. I picked it up and traced its edges with my finger.

"Don't shut me out, Seth. Don't run up the mountain again."

I slipped the white awl into the leather folds of my wallet. I needed to think about her some more.

At six-thirty the doorbell rang. I turned on the porch light and saw Cory smiling from the steps. He was a little thinner, but other than that he hadn't changed since high school. He didn't give me a chance to say hello before he started talking.

"Do you have a minute, Seth?"

"Sure, come in and sit down."

"I'd rather walk down the street, if you don't mind."

"I missed you at the farewell, Cory." I hadn't seen or tried to contact him all summer, but I had called his wife that morning to invite them.

"My wife told me you called, but we couldn't make it."

"That's all right. I'm glad you came by tonight."

"Seth, why didn't you call earlier this summer? You know where we live."

"I guess I've been so busy getting ready for my mission."

"Is that the real reason?"

I thought for a while. "No, Cory, that's not the real reason."

"I didn't think it was. That's why I had to come to talk with you. I don't want you to think I'm a bad person. I want to ask your forgiveness."

"You don't need to do that, Cory."

"Yes I do. When you first got back from school, I thought you'd call or come over. I know we didn't see much of each other during your senior year or this year while you were at the 'Y,' but I still figured you'd try to get ahold of me this summer. When you didn't call, I said to myself, 'You deserve it, Cory. He's going on a mission, and you're married.' Then I realized that I'd never told you how much I appreciated your help that night. At times I wish things were different. I wish I had listened to you. Maybe if none of this had ever happened—but, well, anyway, I hope you can forgive me. I want to be friends again."

"Cory, I'm sorry I didn't call you earlier. It's not because I was mad at you or thought you were bad. It's something else, a feeling I've lost. It's made it hard to see you or Shawn or Andy. It's making it hard to go on a mission and feel worthy to go."

"You've got to feel worthy to go, Seth! You've got to be a great missionary!"

"Why?"

"Your mission can be part mine." He handed me a folded white envelope. "Go ahead. Open it."

I opened the envelope. Inside were two twenty-dollar bills. "Cory, I can't take this money."

"You have to, Seth. I'll send more later."

"But Cory, I have money. You have a wife and children. I don't need it."

"Please! I need to give it. It will keep us in touch. Seth, I love my wife and children, but we started wrong. I'm trying to correct that, to forgive myself, and to regain God's favor. This is part of my road."

I pushed the envelope into my pocket, and we walked back to the house in silence. We exchanged good-byes.

When I got back inside, it was time to go. Mother had finished packing and loading the car. We had a family prayer, and I kissed Jan and Becky good-bye. Mother and I drove to the train station alone. A solitary ticket-taker pushed his pen through a stack of old train schedules, making periodic checks and crosses. Over the huge arch a wooden clock tilted to one side. My new suitcases stood out like polished pennies against the age-worn brown of the benches.

I walked to the ticket counter. "Will the train to Salt Lake be on time?"

"There's a switching problem up the line," he said. "She won't be pulling in for a good three hours."

"Why don't you go on home, Mother. I can wait alone."

"Would you rather?"

"No."

We sat in the stillness of the depot without talking. Then, "Seth, did Cory say something to upset you?"

"No, not really. He just reminded me of something."

I pulled the envelope from my pocket and showed her the money. "He asked me to forgive him."

"Seth? What's bothering you?"

I realized I had shut her out of my life all summer just as I had shut Jaimie out by writing letters that said nothing.

"Why is it so easy to forgive some people and so hard to forgive others? I mean really forgive, so that what they did doesn't matter anymore?"

"Are you thinking of your father?"

"Yes, but it's so much more. Mother, do you remember the rat? Well, it started before that."

I told her all I could remember, from the first presence in Grandpa's garden to the sight of the dark forest. For more than two hours she sat motionless, crying, as I spoke of His closeness to me. I finally told her of the shadeless trees, the hunger and confusion when He withdrew, and His expectation that I love and forgive. I told her of Dad's shoe box of old mementoes. "Why is it so easy to forgive Cory and not my own father? I never thought about not forgiving Cory."

"Cory didn't hurt you like your father did."

"He hurt you, and yet you forgave him."

"I'm not sure I have."

"But you must have, or you couldn't have told us those stories when we were growing up. You couldn't have kept your reasons for the divorce a secret all these years."

"Do you look at it as a secret?"

"Sometimes, but I'm glad you didn't tell me. I'm glad I didn't open the envelopes. I need to forgive, and that means more than leaving the question unanswered. It means more than trips to Salt Lake on the weekends."

"When your father first left me, Jan cried for him one night. I held her in my arms and tried to explain why her daddy would not come home ever again. I began to hate him for what he was doing to her. Jan cried harder. I couldn't comfort her, feeling the way I was feeling. She needed love, not hate. And since there was only one parent to give it, I knew I would have to give more than ever. My heart did not have enough room for both hate and love. I asked the Lord if He would take the bitterness out of my heart so I could raise you in love. He came to me that night and took away the rage and the hurt. It didn't always stay away, but then I would think of you and your sisters, and the anger would ease. If this is forgiveness, then I have forgiven your father."

She put her arm around me, whispering, "You'll learn to forgive him too. I know you—you won't let it rest until it happens."

"I'm not as good as you are, Mother."

"You're better than I am, but you're not as old. Growing older makes things easier, and the gospel has a way of creating an old, wise mind. When you were born and I first held you, I thought, 'This is the first child God gave me after I stopped rebelling.' I didn't want you to do what I did. I gave you a name and asked God to honor that name. 'And God revealed himself unto Seth, and he rebelled not, but offered an acceptable sacrifice . . .' Give Him the sacrifice, Seth. That's why He withdrew."

The ticket-taker tapped my shoulder. "There's your train, son."

I hugged my mother and kissed her. A porter took my suitcases from me and disappeared into the dark. "I feel so alone, Mother—like the first night He left me."

"Then remember the two disciples who walked with Christ on the road to Emmaus."

I followed the porter into the dark of the train. I sat down next to the window and watched the lights of home slip into the distance as the train moved into the desert toward Utah. When the last lights disappeared, the train was wrapped in darkness. I tried to sleep and put the questions out of my mind, but the rhythm of the train seemed to parade them by me.

The train twisted through the foothills. I pushed my face against the glass, trying to see ahead through the night, but the darkness was total, and loneliness settled in heavily. I bowed my head.

"Father, I can't control my feelings. I can't force love and forgiveness into my heart, as much as I want to. Is it so important, Father? I want to, but I can't determine the way I feel or whom I love."

The darkness seemed to lift in the corner of the train car. Somebody stepped through the wall. The copper bracelets rattled as he adjusted the old sweat-soaked hat to his head.

Ride, Seth. Pick up the reins. Let go of the saddle horn and ride!

"I can't Uncle Morgan! I'm afraid!"

Pick up the reins, Seth. Let go.

But he was changing. He was growing taller and taller. He stared at me with eyes sunk deep into their sockets. Long fingers stretched toward me, pushing the smell into my face.

Give me some paper, Seth. Let me make you that helicopter.

"You can't, Uncle Jens. You're dying."

Help me, Seth. I can't fold the paper—my hands are shaking.

"You're dying, Uncle Jens. You're dying!"

Now he too changed, shrank. He cowered on the floor, shielding his head.

They're beating me, Seth. They're hurting me! Get them off my back!

"Don't learn to fight, Mark."

I've got to fight. They're going to beat me.

"You're losing, Mark—they're still beating you."

No, I'm winning. I know how to fight.

He buried his face in his hands. An M-16 lay on the floor of the train, and the walls became jungles.

Seth, I have to shoot him.

"Pray, Andy. He'll help you."

He won't help me. I'm going to shoot him. I hate him. I hate them all!

"Stop hating, Andy."

I can't stop. They won't let me.

He grabbed his stomach in pain and rocked back and forth in the aisle.

"Are you hurt, Cory? Why are you crying?"

It hurts. Why does it hurt when you're wrong?

"Maybe He doesn't cause the hurt. Do you love her?"

I don't even know what that means.

The darkness diffused into the twinkling of many lights. Jaimie stood with the tiny lights of Temple Square shining in her hair.

The knots are getting tighter, Seth. I can't undo them, but I tried. I tried, Seth.

"Jaimie, I—"

But she was gone.

"Grandpa can undo the knots. He knows the scriptures. Grandpa, my eyes are closed. Teach me what to see."

Open your eyes this time, Seth. You're sliding just like cousin Lauritz.

"Keep me from sliding!"

Go to your father, Seth. Help him.

"I need help, Grandpa!"

We must think of them. We must not be selfish. Go to your father.

"I don't have a father anymore. I lost my father. He left me. He's not coming back. Don't you leave me too, Grandpa."

But he was gone. Only the darkness of the train and the noise of the wheels against the tracks remained. I searched for Him, but He didn't return. They all came back but Him.

23

The Highest Reach

When the train pulled into Salt Lake City, I knew what I had to do. Love wasn't only a feeling, it was a decision. I pulled out one of Jaimie's letters and found her phone number. Her mother answered and put Jaimie on.

"Seth, where are you?"

"In Salt Lake, the train station."

We exchanged the typical greetings. Then she hesitantly asked, "Isn't this kind of foolish?"

"Jaimie, I don't have much time. I'm carrying your awl again. Is that okay? I'm not asking you to wait for me. I can't—that's not fair for either of us, but I'll write. Not letters like this summer."

"Seth, I'm still wearing the mouse."

A few minutes later we hung up. The next phone call would be more difficult. I called the school where my father taught and asked the secretary to have him call me at the pay-phone number when he got out. I sat on my suitcases for forty-five minutes until the phone rang.

"Dad," I started, "I just got in from California. I have to report to the mission home sometime today. I want to talk to you."

"I'm in school all day, Seth."

"I can wait till this afternoon."

"What do you need to see me about?"

"It's hard to say over the phone. Will you come?"

"Where are you?"

"I'm at the station now, but I'm walking up to the temple. I'll be there when you get out of school."

"I'll meet you at four o'clock at the north gate."

The clouds that had been threatening all afternoon suddenly broke, and it began to pour. The rain was so heavy that it obscured the massive gray walls of the temple. The trees lining the main walks merged with the gray misting waves of rain.

I entered the iron gate on North Temple, crossed over to the visitor's center, and waited in the entrance. The square was completely deserted. Isolated puddles formed here and there, then overflowed and pushed down the crevices to the lawn. The only sounds I could hear were the pounding of the rain on the roof and the banging of the ropes against the flagpole.

I waited for forty-five minutes. Over and over again I tried to plan what to say, but the questions never took form. I just stood hunched in my overcoat staring at the trees and the temple, glancing every minute at the north gate, thinking about nothing at all.

At twenty after four, he came. He stood by the gate holding a black pearl-handled umbrella over his head. The water poured down its sides, splashing onto his shoes. The collar of his overcoat was turned up, and his free hand was buried in a pocket.

I stepped from the entranceway and walked toward him. Rain began to run off my hair before I reached him. I pointed to one of the many tabernacle doorways and ran for its cover.

I scrambled into the doorway out of the rain. My father walked across the sidewalk past the planters that surrounded the temple. He stepped into the opposite corner of the doorway, leaned against the stonework, and shook the rain off the umbrella. He hadn't looked at me yet.

"Thanks for coming, Dad. It's miserable weather."

"Yes, it is."

"I'm sorry you got your shoes all wet."

It was a stupid thing to say, but it ended the drumming of the rain. He shook his head and smiled the tight-lipped smile I had first noticed when he had taken us to Lagoon.

"Seth, let me make things easier for you."

He glanced at me for a brief second, then turned back to stare at the temple.

"I called your mother after talking to you. I think she was more surprised than I was. She told me what to expect. I hope you won't feel she broke any trust by telling me. I didn't want to come here unprepared. I almost didn't come, but I'm here now. Ask me your questions."

He stared straight ahead, his body rigid and his lips pressed tightly together.

"Dad, I don't know what I want to know. Maybe if I tell you how I feel, then we can talk without any barriers. I want that."

"You go ahead, Seth, and I'll listen."

"For as long as I can remember, your absence has influenced my life. I didn't always realize it was you, but now I know it was true. My life has been a search for you, Dad, from my first memory till now. I used to think I was looking for manhood or acceptance from my friends. I bounced from thing to thing and person to person, each time thinking I'd found what I was after, but each time something was still missing. When I was little, I tried to find it in men like Grandpa and Uncle Morgan. The Lord tried to keep me from grabbing the wrong things as so many others had, but I kept trying. I tried to be Grandpa's son. I tried to be Uncle Morgan's son. I tried to be God's son. In a way they were all fathers to me. But I'm your son too, Dad. That's why I've never found what I wanted anywhere else. Then God left me so I could keep growing. I want to love you, Dad, but I have to accept you and forgive you."

I stopped for a moment. I looked at my father staring straight ahead in the rain without a trace of emotion on his face. I bit the inside of my cheek to stop the trembling in my voice. "Dad, help me to love you."

He turned the collar of his coat up against his neck and buried his hands deeper into his pockets. When he finally spoke, his voice was so low I almost lost it in the rain.

"I always loved your mother. I met her in high school when we lived in Ogden. Neither one of us had any real convictions in those days. We wanted what the world could give, not the things God wanted. I tried to want them—for years I tried, but other things kept getting in the way. I prayed for answers—they never came. Your mother was the same.

"When I turned nineteen, I went on a mission because it would have broken my father's heart if I didn't, and I thought it might help me to want the right things. My heart was never in it. I wanted to come home and marry your mother the whole two years. I asked her the first day back. She turned me down. She didn't want to be tied down by marriage. There was too much in life to see and do. I couldn't accept her answer. I pestered her and hounded her until finally she agreed to the marriage as long as she could live her life the way she wanted. I agreed, and we drove to Nevada that night.

"As soon as we had a little money, we moved to San Francisco. There we found all the excitement we both wanted. For a while it looked as though everything would work. We left the Church completely, dropping all the standards we'd fought against all our lives.

"Neither one of us wanted children then. We both knew they would get in the way. Then the war broke out, and I was sent to the Pacific for two years. When I came home, nothing was the same. I tried to live the life we used to, the only life we could share, but she had drawn away from me during the war. We talked of divorce. I thought if we had children maybe they would hold us together, but your mother still didn't want any. I was a medical student, and she believed what I said about certain drugs. It worked twice before she realized I was lying to her, and your two sisters were born. They held us together for a few more years while I finished medical school. Neither one of us changed, though.

"I finally finished medical school, and we moved to southern California. When we started to drift again, I got active in the Church. I had seen families pull together in the mission field and hoped it would work for us, too. I thought if I could get your mother to marry me in the temple, we could stay together. I tried to straighten up my life and began to force your mother to listen to me read the scriptures. And it worked. I know she's told you that story. She changed overnight. A short while later we came here, to this temple, and were married. She wanted another child, and you were born. Everything I wanted had come true.

"Then what went wrong? I hadn't changed as she had. I still wanted the other life. For two years I tried to live in two worlds, but it drove me crazy. During those years, your mother got closer and closer to the Lord and the Church. She was moving ahead, and I was slipping more and more each day. I knew I would not be a good father for you or your sisters."

He stopped and drew his breath in deeply, holding it inside before pushing it out in a broken sigh. And then the tears came, and his face showed emotion for the first time. The wall was breaking, and suddenly I didn't know if I wanted to look behind it. The rain forced us deeper into the alcove. He fought for control.

"Please, I can't tell you all I did during those years. I want to help you, but if you could love me without knowing everything—"

He stopped again and wiped his face with his handkerchief.

"I struggled to live right, to do what God wanted me to do. I couldn't. The struggle made me rebellious, and I was losing your mother, this time to God. She sensed it and tried to help me. She knew how hard it was to give up everything, but it was no good. I knew that sooner or later I would pull her down because she was still fighting the pull of the other life too. Your sister Jan was five, and I was affecting her also. I knew your mother had chosen the better life. I knew she would be able to live that life if I weren't there. So I left.

I never came back. We got a civil divorce, and two years later they annulled the temple marriage. I went back to school and got a teaching degree. I've lived in Salt Lake ever since.

"I know I haven't done anything for you over the years. I didn't want to influence you. I was afraid if I spent more time with you, you would learn the wrong things. I suppose I was ashamed, too. It was easier to let your mother take care of everything. Then you came to school, and I saw you were strong enough. I looked forward to those weekends we spent together."

Once again he stopped and looked into the rain. The wind picked up the rope against the flagpole, driving the rain in waves across the temple.

"I wouldn't blame you if you hated me, Seth, for what I've done to your life. I have always been grateful to your mother for telling you only the good things. There were so few of them. I don't expect you to love me. It is enough that you have shared some of your life with me this year. I haven't changed over the years, Seth. Your life has been hard because of my decision, but it would have been worse had I stayed with your mother. Leaving was the best thing I ever did for you. Maybe this will help you to forgive me. I didn't love you enough to change for you, but I loved you enough to live without you."

He sagged in his coat and looked down at his rain-splashed shoes. I wanted to put my arms around him and cry with him, but I couldn't. I was ashamed that I'd made him relive it, and the shame was intense. All I could feel was pity, and pity seemed a long way from love or forgiveness.

"Dad, I'm sorry. I'm sorry for you and for mother. I'm sorry for all of us. I shouldn't have asked you to come today. I wanted to tell you that I love you, that I could forgive you. I wanted us to understand each other."

I couldn't control the tears, and turned to face the corner of the doorway. I felt his hand rest on my shoulder. It lay there for a second or two, then gripped me hard before he finally spoke.

"I've lied to myself all these years. I didn't really love you, did I? I loved myself. Had I loved myself less I could have loved you more. Maybe you've been like me, Seth, in that one way? And that's probably my fault. I influenced you anyway. I've fought that truth all my life. I don't want to face it now. It's easier to live with a lie than face it. It's the one battle nobody wants to fight. It will be too convenient to hide behind my lies again when you're gone. But you'll conquer it, Seth. You'll face that truth. You'll forgive me and love me because you'll forget yourself. You're your mother's son, not mine.

"I'm proud of you for wanting to love me enough to go through what you're going through. I may be too full of self-love to give you much in return, but I love you, Seth. You will be a better man than I am. You'll honor me even though I don't deserve it.

"When I die, I'm going to go to the Lord with empty hands. I have nothing to offer Him, not even love. He's always been a stranger to me, someone who avoided me, and I avoided Him. But knowing that my son will go to Him with his hands full, knowing that my son knew Him as a Father, will make my shame bearable, and maybe I can hold my head a little higher."

I reached up and placed my hand on his. I felt his other hand cover mine, press it, and rub it awkwardly before he pulled both hands away. I heard the rain pelting the top of his umbrella as he stepped away from the tabernacle. His footsteps echoed down the sidewalk and faded. I pressed my face against the wood of the door and waited for control to return.

The feel of his hand on mine still lay softly on my shoulder. I turned to the temple and knelt on the wet pavement.

"Father, I need You. Don't stay in Your heavens. I need You to tell me the answers as You always have before. How can I make this sacrifice?"

I looked at the temple and waited. There was something on the wall that I noticed for the first time. Tiny granite stars were chiseled on the side of the temple, halfway to the spires that reached higher above them. And then came the whisper, *There is the past. There are memories.*

The rich, clean memories shone and quivered inside, piling deeper and deeper until they rose like little starpoints in a night of confusion to point the way. And now there was a new memory—his hand on my shoulder. It wouldn't replace the face that couldn't be there, but they stood side by side.

You have begun. Now reach.

"Did You walk by my side so I could know the answer in my own life as it came from You? Is it within my reach? Within his reach? Within the reach of us all? Higher than manhood?"

High enough to cast your own shadow.

The deeper meaning of His words found a holding place. I felt His smile for one brief moment as He held me within the peace of His Spirit.